D0980835

SPACER DREAMS

LARRY SEGRIFF

BAEN

SPACER DREAMS

This is a work of fiction. All the characters and events portrayed in this book are fictional, and any resemblance to real people or incidents is purely coincidental.

A Baen Books Original

Baen Publishing Enterprises
P.O. Box 1403
Riverdale, NY 10471

ISBN: 0-671-87696-1

Cover art by Stephen Hickman

First printing, November 1995

Distributed by Simon & Schuster
1230 Avenue of the Americas
New York, NY 10020

Typeset by Windhaven Press, Auburn, NH
Printed in the United States of America

To my wife, Marlys, for her constant love, support, and encouragement

I would also like to thank
Ed Gorman and Marty Greenberg,
without whom this book
would never have been written.

Chapter One

The clank of heavy boots on steel deck plates resounded in my ears. Around me, ten veterans, all in the light blue Space Guard pressure suits, checked their weapons one last time. If our informant was correct, we were closing in on the pirates' headquarters.

Perhaps this would be the day we caught him, Old Jack himself, if Finagle's Lady was with us.

It was crowded in the bay where we sat, strapped in to our seats, red warning lights blinking overhead, but the members of my team were all relaxed. They were experienced Guardsmen, professionals through and through, and though I knew I looked young to them, I was in command, and they would follow where I led.

The retros fired. I could feel the ship turn, feel the first ghostly fingers of gravity begin to tug at me after more than seventy-two hours in space. Yes, perhaps this would be the day.

"Mr. Jenkins, do you have an answer for us?" Mr. Forrester's sharp, strident voice cut sharply across my daydream, pulling me out of the glory of the Guard and back to the dull, dreary confines of school.

There were no jauntily-clad pirates here, nor any blue Guardsmen uniforms; just the drab grey jumpsuits of my classmates, each with the distinctive Brighthome patch on the left shoulder.

Before me, Mr. Forrester stood patiently. He was a commanding figure, trim and muscular, with his greying black hair cut short and his salt-and-pepper mustache neatly trimmed. I could see Mr. Forrester as a pirate—or as a Guardsman, for that matter—but of course he wasn't. He was just a teacher here at the Brighthome Youth Center.

"Uh, yes, sir," I stammered, rising automatically to my feet. The largest part of me was still on deck with the rest of the Guard. "Uh, Fomalhaut IV, sir." That was the name of the planet we'd been about to land on.

I heard snickers from most of my classmates, and knew I'd gotten it wrong again.

"Fomalhaut IV," Mr. Forrester said. "I see. Very interesting." He liked to wear these horn-rimmed spectacles, even though we all knew his vision was fine. Everybody's vision was fine. But they did make him look more ferocious when he scowled.

He was scowling now as he added, "Mr. Jenkins, I would like you to stay behind after class. There are some things we need to discuss."

A loud, "Ooooh," went up from about three quarters of my class. When Mr. Forrester asked you to stay after, it meant big trouble. In my case, it probably meant that I'd lose my shuttle privileges for a week. Again.

I nodded. "Yes, sir," I mumbled. Darn it, he knew how important those shuttle flights were to me.

Sinking back in my chair, I tried not to notice the smirks on most people's faces. Only Jamie, my best friend, looked at me with anything like sympathy. Jamie, and one other, someone I hadn't expected to understand.

There was a new girl in our class. She'd joined us just the day before. I didn't even know her name, but as I slid back into my seat I was surprised by the expression on her face: sadness, and something that I could only call understanding.

She looked away quickly, though, before I could even be sure I'd seen anything.

For the rest of the class, I couldn't think of anything but her. Fortunately, Mr. Forrester didn't call on me again.

"I don't understand you, Mr. Jenkins."

Class was over. The others had all gone, some of them to dinner; most of them to the rec area. Jamie, I knew, would be at the caves, waiting for me.

The room looked smaller, somehow, without them in it. The fifteen student desks were arranged in a large circle, with Mr. Forrester's desk nearest the door. His was larger than ours, and made of wood, but had the same small keyboard and display built into the top surface. His display was still turned on, and I could see that he'd called up my file.

There was something archaic about Mr. Forrester, with his horn-rimmed glasses and his wooden desk. With some people, that might have seemed odd, or even comic; with Mr. Forrester, it seemed appropriate, and awfully intimidating. Especially when, as now, he stood behind that massive desk, looking out over the tops of those horn-rims, and scowled.

"I have to tell you, Mr. Jenkins, you're the brightest kid in your class, maybe one of the brightest who's ever come here, but you're wasting all that. Dreaming in class. Not paying attention. Not *learning* anything." He paused, but his gaze didn't soften. "Tell me," he went on after a moment, "what do you plan on doing when you leave here?"

I didn't want to answer that. For one thing, if anyone ever found out, I would be the laughing-stock of the whole school. Even more than I already was. For another, I didn't want to jinx it. I knew it wasn't logical, but there was a part of me that was sure that as long as I never spoke it out loud, there was a chance my dream might come true. Telling someone, however, would spoil it.

"I don't know, sir," I said, which was as close to a lie as I would ever let myself get.

"You don't know." His voice told me that he didn't believe me. He didn't press it, though. "Well, Mr. Jenkins, I have a feeling that you'll have more opportunities available to you than most kids who come here, but you won't take advantage of them by daydreaming. You've got potential, son. Don't waste it. Otherwise, your entire future will be no better than this place."

With one hand, he indicated the grey, desolate landscape beyond the window.

"It will, sir," I said softly. "I promise you, it will be better than this."

He looked at me steadily for a moment, then gave a single, sharp nod. "Prove it." And then he sat down and started working. A couple of keystrokes and my file disappeared, replaced with a series of equations.

I was dismissed.

I had a lot to think about as I headed out to the caves beyond the school. The ground was dusty, the air just a touch cooler than was comfortable, but that was the way it always was on Brighthome.

Off to my left, in the rec area, I saw a group of a dozen or so kids. As usual, they were alone, with no teacher around to supervise them. There weren't many opportunities for mischief on Brighthome, and as long as there weren't a lot of fights or incidents of vandalism or things like that, the overworked staff here pretty much left the kids alone outside of the classrooms. Oh, we had our Sunday meals together, and there were scheduled activities in the evenings and on weekends, but those were more to make the place look good to outsiders. In reality, the teachers and supervisors spent as little time with most of the students as they could.

The kids over in the rec area—they looked to be about fifteen or sixteen, most of them—were clustered around one bigger kid. Burles. I didn't know his first name; everyone—even the teachers—simply called him Burles. He was my age, nearly an adult, and I'd always felt he was exactly the kind of kid Brighthome was intended to help—and exactly the kind of kid who would never let it help him. He was tough, independent, and too darn proud to let anyone help him, and if his future was nothing better than a prison cell, well, at least it was *his* future.

Fritz Laramie, a fifteen-year-old who was big for

his age, but nowhere near as big as Burles, walked past them. Burles called out to him, and I saw Fritz's shoulders stiffen before he turned. I knew what was going to happen next, and though I didn't want to watch I couldn't seem to tear my eyes away.

Burles and his group surrounded Fritz, and then Burles said something. Fritz shook his head. Burles said something else, and again Fritz shook his head. Then, so fast that I could hardly see it, Burles' right hand shot out and struck Fritz across the face. Fritz stumbled back a step and this time, when Burles said something, Fritz's shoulders sagged and then he nodded.

Burles' message was clear: follow me, or regret it. Leadership by fear and intimidation.

I shook my head and made sure I steered a wide path around the rec area as I continued on to the caves.

"So how'd it go?" Jamie demanded as soon as I walked in.

My light picked him up, leaning against the stalagmite we called "The Fang." Our campsite was deeper in, but this was where I'd figured I'd find him. This was just far enough in to be out of range of the snoopers, and it was a good, comfortable place to wait. Snoopers were listening devices the teachers sometimes used to eavesdrop on the students. The rock walls of the caves interfered with them. I figured the administration probably had some other way to monitor what went on deeper in, but I tended not to think about that much. For one thing, I really didn't think they used it very often. After all, Jamie and I weren't troublemakers. Watching us would get boring fast, and no one else ever came into these caves. Beyond that, though, I tended not to think about it because I didn't want to. Brighthome was a detention center, the worst in the galaxy, and privacy here was both rare and precious—even if it was only an illusion.

I shrugged. "About like you'd expect."

"Did he take away your shuttle privileges?"

"No, and that was odd. He didn't lay any punishment on me at all. Just told me I was 'wasting myself,' and that I should try to do better. And you know what, Jamie? He was right. We are wasting ourselves."

Jamie laughed. He was a little guy, only a little over a meter and a half tall—and that was with his boots on—with this bright red hair and a lot of freckles all over. He had a great laugh, though. Even if I was mad, hearing him always made me want to laugh, too.

"Hey, buddy," he said, "you forget where we are? I mean, it's not like we asked to come here, remember? This is Brighthome."

I smiled faintly. "Yeah, I know, Jamie." Our eyes met, and then together we said, "Penal Colony to the Stars." That's how we'd always thought of it. It sounded more glamorous, like something that Old Jack himself might once have broken out of. Certainly a lot better than "Brighthome Youth Center."

Lately, though, I'd found myself thinking along other lines. The official brochure on this place described it as a "last chance for the Galaxy's troubled youth," and I was starting to agree with that. As far as I knew, there had never been a Guardsman from Brighthome, but if the literature could be believed, if this really was a "last chance," then maybe I could be the first.

Maybe my secret dream really could come true.

"Come on," Jamie said, jumping up and slugging me on the shoulder. "I got a new vid game today. Let's go play it." And he dashed off deeper into the caves.

I grinned and shook my head, but I followed him, Mr. Forrester's words still echoing in my mind.

Chapter Two

"Mother!"

I came swimming up out of sleep, the echoes of my own voice ringing in my ears. I knew what it was, of course: that dream again. Quietly, I looked around the darkened barracks, hoping that I had only cried out in my mind.

No one else stirred, and I slowly let out a sigh of relief. Swinging my legs over the side of my bed, I dropped softly down to the floor. I had the top bunk, and a quick drop like that was less noisy than the rickety old ladder.

Checking the bunk below me, I saw that Jamie was fast asleep. I felt a soft smile touch my lips as I saw his tousled red hair peeking out from beneath the covers. He was a heck of a friend, even if he did spend too much time playing games and dreaming of being a pirate.

Still smiling, I pulled on my clothes and my boots,

padded softly over to the door and let myself out. It would be a long time before I could get back to sleep, I knew. Might as well take in some night air. The Prefects—that's what they called the dorm monitors here on Brighthome—had already come by at lights out. Things had been pretty quiet lately, and so the Precepts were only rarely making their random bed checks. I figured I was pretty safe sneaking off for a time. And I needed to.

I'd had that dream, off and on, for as long as I could remember. Not that that was all that long. My memories only went back four years, and most of them were all about Brighthome. Before that, before I woke up in a survival pod with the Guard all around me, I had no memories at all.

In the dream, I was in a small, dark, enclosed space. I couldn't see anything, but I had the impression that the walls were grey, and that I should know where I was. Outside the space I was in, I could hear male voices, talking. The words were muffled, their meaning unclear, but their tone was unmistakably menacing. I didn't know who they were, but I knew they were bad guys, and not like the ones in Jamie's games, either. These were for real, and they were looking for me.

That's all. The dream always ends right there. I'm alone, scared, in the dark—and I want my mother. It always seems that I'm more frightened for her than for me. And when I wake up, her name on my lips, it's always with a sense of sadness that I can't explain.

The cold air bit at me and it felt good. I still had that sense of confinement on me, and the wide open space around me was comforting. If only I could throw off that inexplicable sadness as easily.

Above me, Antillus hung low in the sky, a mottled green banana that looked about ready for picking. I'd seen it in all its phases over the years, and though it was a beautiful planet, the sight of it only served to make me feel even more lost. What hung in the sky over my home? I wondered. And who had first pointed it out to me?

There was a weight in my heart that pulled my gaze down to the ground and kept it there as I walked so that I didn't see her until her voice spoke out of the night.

"I hear you're pirate kin."

I looked up, startled, to see that my feet had taken me off campus and over toward the mouth of our cave. She was seated on some rocks off to one side, the new girl I'd seen in class that morning.

"That's what they say," I replied. I wanted to keep on walking, to go off by myself and think, but I couldn't. Not without seeming rude, and with the type of people who lived on Brighthome, you tried not to make anyone mad. At least, not until you knew why they'd been sent here.

"I've always wanted to meet a real pirate," she said. She smiled when she said it, though, and in the faint, green light from Antillus I couldn't tell if she was joking or sincere.

I couldn't think of anything to say to that so I just nodded my head and started to walk off.

"Wait," she said, and I was surprised to hear a softer note in her voice.

"Yes?" I turned back to her.

"Do you have a minute? I—I guess I'd just like someone to talk to."

I nodded, recognizing what I was seeing. She'd been here, what? Two days? Three at the most, I figured, just long enough for that initial brashness to wear off and the fear to kick in. Another few days and she'd be her old self—whatever that was—but right now she was vulnerable and afraid.

Just like me.

"Sure," I said, coming over and taking a seat on a rock near hers. "What do you want to talk about?"

"Oh, I don't know," she shrugged. "They say you've been here the longest. Is that true?"

I nodded. "Except for some of the teachers. I came here when I was thirteen. Most kids don't come to Brighthome before they're fourteen or fifteen."

She looked at me steadily for a moment. "Yeah, that makes sense. It would take that long to make it through the system of foster homes and other juvenile centers. So what was so special in your case? Were you really a pirate?"

I chuckled, though inwardly I didn't find this at all amusing. I'd learned it was a lot safer talking to people who thought they knew all about me. I could usually just stay silent and let them think what they wanted. "That's me," I said, "Long John Jenkins."

She didn't smile back. "No, really, I'm curious. I'd like to know."

I couldn't hold her gaze any longer. I swung my eyes up toward Antillus and felt that old weight settle in on my heart. "Seriously?" I asked.

"Seriously," she said.

"Then you first. Tell me who you are and how you got here. Then I'll tell you."

I wondered if she'd go for it. You never knew, and for a moment it looked like she wasn't going to. Then she said, "I got into some trouble on Arcturus IV—"

"Stop," I said, holding up my hand. "Everyone's here because they 'got into some trouble.' If you want my life story, you'll have to do better than that."

She was silent again and I turned to look at her. Like me, she had turned her gaze skyward, no longer looking at me. This was the first chance I'd had to really look at her, and I was surprised at how pretty she was. Her hair was brown and not quite shoulder length, and she seemed to be about my age, but mostly what I liked about her was this air of strength she had that set her apart from most of the kids that came here.

She continued looking out at the stars and I found myself wondering what she was looking for, or who.

"All right." Her voice was even softer, making it hard to read whatever emotions lay within it. She turned to look at me and said, "My name's Michaela, but I go by Mikey, and if you laugh I'll punch you right in the nose, I swear it."

"I'm not laughing," I said. "Pleased to meet you, Mikey," and I meant it.

She held my gaze for a long moment before dropping it and looking to the night sky again. As she turned, her hair fell across her face and she made an annoyed, sweeping gesture to brush it aside. "I really did get in trouble on Arcturus IV," she said, "but it wasn't any big deal. I mean, I didn't swipe anything, or sell something I shouldn't have. It's just that I wasn't supposed to be there. I—I kind of ran away from home a few years ago. I got caught there, on Arcturus IV, trying to land a job with an ID that wasn't mine."

"And for that you got sent here? Come on, Mikey. There must be more to it than that."

She nodded. "I'm from Markus Colony."

Which explained a lot, actually. Markus Colony was very strict. They didn't consider their people citizens until they'd turned twenty-five, and you couldn't get married there until you were thirty. Markus Colony turned out some of the best educated, most productive workers in the galaxy, but not many people wanted to live there.

"I see," I said.

"And that's not all." She paused, apparently searching for the right words. "My father's a Senator," she went on. "He felt, with his position and all, that it was necessary to make an example of me. To show, I guess, that no one is above the law. So he put in a word and got me sent here."

I didn't know what to say, so as usual I didn't say anything at all. After a moment she gave a small shrug and turned back to me. "So that's my story. I've bummed around on a few different planets— seen quite a bit of the galaxy, actually, but I didn't exactly go first class. Nothing like what you pirates have done, huh?"

She was smiling when she said it, but I didn't smile back.

"I'm not a pirate," I said. Something about the pain in her story had touched me, and for the first time in quite a while I found myself wanting to tell someone the truth. "At least, I don't think I am. I was found floating in space when I was a kid, alone. I had no ID and no memory and no one came forth to claim me. On top of that, the ship I was on bore no registry and there was no log, nothing to even indicate what world it had come from. The Guardsmen who found me tried to identify me, but it was no use. They had nothing to go on. In the end, I was sent here. No one really thought I was a pirate's kid, but nothing else made sense, and I've heard this is the cheapest youth center in the sector."

"Wow." I had no idea whether she knew how rare it was for someone to get this story or not—even Jamie didn't know as much as I'd just told her and he'd been my best friend for two years. She seemed impressed, though. I took that as a good sign.

"So you have no idea who you are? You could turn out to be the President's son or something!"

I laughed. "Hardly. I mean, I've been here four years. If my parents had been important, surely someone would have come for me by now. No, whoever they were, I'm certain they were just little people who got caught in a bad situation."

"You mean like a hijacking?"

I nodded. For something that was theoretically impossible, space piracy happened quite a lot. "It would explain everything," I said.

"But what about your memories?" she asked. "Pirates don't normally leave mindless kids behind, do they?"

"No," I said. "They don't. But no other explanation makes sense."

"There is one," she started, but I cut her off.

"Don't say it. Don't even think it." Brainwipe was the ugliest word I knew, and not only because it just might have happened to me. It was the worst form of punishment, something society only did in the most extreme cases. Brainwipe was irreversible. And if that's what had happened, if some pirates had wanted to test out a new method for doing it, say, and used me as their guinea pig, then it meant my memories, my family, my entire life before Brighthome were completely and utterly lost. And I just couldn't believe that. I had to hold on to the hope that my memories were there, somewhere, merely waiting for the right cues to bring them out again.

"It wasn't that," I said, as though hoping could make it true. "I know it wasn't."

She only nodded and dropped her gaze to the rocks at her feet.

"So what's Brighthome like?" she asked after the silence had stretched for a bit.

Again, I surprised myself by answering honestly. "Lonely," I said.

She looked at me, startled. "You're not what I expected, Mr. Jenkins."

"Please," I said. "Mr. Forrester calls me mister. My friends call me Tom."

Now she smiled, and I was pleased to see how pretty it made her. "Oh? And am I your friend, Tom?"

"I think so, Mikey," I said. "I think so."

She didn't say anything to that, but I didn't mind. Silence could be comfortable at times, especially on Brighthome.

"So," she said after a moment, "you didn't answer my question. What's Brighthome like?"

Actually, I had answered her question, as honestly as I could. It just wasn't the answer she was looking for.

I shrugged. "You know the stats, I'm sure. One

hundred fifty kids, all of whom have passed through various foster homes and care centers, and all of whom were deemed incorrigible. Not bad kids, most of them, not necessarily the galaxy's worst, just the ones the system couldn't help. Brighthome itself was an abandoned mining colony when they decided to put a youth center here." I grinned. "Jamie and I call it the Penal Colony to the Stars."

She smiled, too, but sobered quickly. "That's a description of what this place *is*, Tom. I want to know what it's *like*."

I shrugged again. "Pretty much as you've seen it. You go to class during the day, attend a lecture or a 'structured leisure activity' in the evening, maybe do some groundskeeping on the weekends. After a while, if you're good, you can earn some special privileges. Like flying. Beyond that, the teachers basically leave us alone."

"They do?" She seemed surprised. Me, I'd gotten so used to it that I took it for granted.

"Sure," I said. "Keep in mind, we're the ones the system has given up on. All they have to do is keep us out of trouble until we turn eighteen, and their job is done."

"Doesn't sound too bad," she said.

"It's not. Like I said, as long as we don't cause trouble—and by trouble I mean anything that makes them fill out reports or look bad to Central Admin —the teachers pretty much leave us alone. Besides, I suspect that Brighthome doesn't exactly attract the brightest and the best."

"Burnouts, huh?"

I nodded. "There's a pretty good student-to-teacher ratio here, but considering who the teachers are, that doesn't mean much." There was more to it than that, but I didn't want to bring it up. The truth was that I probably had a slightly different view of the place than most kids. I wasn't sure, but I suspected I had more freedom, and more privileges, than just about anyone else. After all, I hadn't been sent here because of my record. I didn't want to say that, though. I didn't want to sound like I thought I was better than the others. In particular, I didn't want to sound like I thought I was better than her.

She thought about what I'd said, but didn't seem particularly surprised by it. I wondered what kind of reputation Brighthome had out there among the stars.

"And the kids?" she asked. "What are they like?"

I shook my head. "You're better off on your own. There are a couple of cliques around; stay away from them. They'll only get you into trouble, and you don't look like you'll be here all that long. As for the rest, it's different for everyone here. Some get along with most of the teachers, some get into trouble all the time, and the rest of us just get by." I looked at her and grinned. "I don't know why, but somehow I don't think you'll just get by."

She didn't grin back. She just deflected my comment back at me. "And you, Tom? What do you do? After all, the teachers must know your background, don't they?"

So much for avoiding that question. I looked back toward green Antillus as I thought about what Mr. Forrester had said earlier. "I don't know," I said. "To be honest, I doubt many of them care enough to look up individual students' records."

"So you just get by, then?" she pressed.

I nodded. "On a good day, Mikey. On a good day."

There must have been something in my voice because she didn't ask me any more questions. We watched the stars in silence for a while, and then I headed back to my bunk and a few hours sleep.

Chapter Three

Morning broke much earlier than I wanted. What with staying up late playing games with Jamie, not sleeping well because of my dream, and then talking with Mikey for over an hour, I was pretty tired, but I had to get up. This was Brighthome, after all, not the Galactic Hilton. Besides, today was Friday, which meant physics in the morning, my favorite subject.

Blearily, I stumbled off to the sonic showers to start my day.

"Do you have an answer for us, Mr. Jenkins?" Mr. Forrester's voice thundered across my dreams, snapping me out of my light doze. He was the astronomy teacher on Tuesdays and Thursdays and the physics instructor on Mondays, Wednesdays, and Fridays.

"Uh, yes, sir," I stammered. The ragtag ends of

his question were echoing in my ear, and for once I knew the answer. "F equals M A," I said.

His eyes touched mine and locked for a moment, and then he smiled gently. "That is correct, Mr. Jenkins. Very good." Then he lifted his gaze and addressed the entire class. "F equals M A is the basic equation for everything we'll be talking about in this class. Force equals Mass times Acceleration. It was Newton's second law of motion and it remains as true, as potent, and as ubiquitous today as it was all those years ago." He paused, then added, "If you're ever at a loss for an answer in this class, say that. F equals M A. You've got a good chance of being right." He looked at me as he said that, and smiled.

I glanced over at Mikey. She wasn't looking at me, which allowed me to admire again how pretty she looked. She was wearing a black jumpsuit— everyone at Brighthome wore jumpsuits. It wasn't a uniform or anything, but they were the most comfortable and the most convenient clothing around. In fact, they were the only clothing sold over in the PX. Our biggest choice was whether to wear black, blue, grey, red, or green.

Most kids wore grey, because the rock dust didn't show as much and so they could go longer between cleanings. I preferred blue, myself, but the black looked good on her. It went well with her shining, dark hair and her flashing, dark eyes. Even as I watched, almost as if she felt my eyes upon her, she reached up and rather jerkily brushed back some hair that had fallen across her face. Then she looked up, met my gaze, and gave me a little grin.

I smiled back, already liking the way this day was shaping up.

❖　❖　❖

Class went all the way up till lunchtime. I didn't have to answer any more questions for Mr. Forrester, but I didn't fall asleep again, either. When the bell rang, I shut down my display and fairly leaped out of my seat. I was hoping to walk Mikey over to the cafeteria, but Mr. Forrester called to me as I was heading toward the door.

"Mr. Jenkins," he said. "I'd like a word with you."

Mikey glanced over at me, gave me a rueful smile, and then followed the others out. I watched her leave, then turned back to Mr. Forrester, careful to keep my feelings off my face.

"I see you've thought about our last conversation, Mr. Jenkins," he said. "That's good. I told you you've got potential, son, and I meant it." He went around his desk but didn't call anything up on his display. "Mr. Jenkins—Tom—I'd like to be able to help you. You've got a chance to make something of yourself, and I'd like to see that happen. I have some connections that reach beyond Brighthome. If you'd like a recommendation from me, or if you'd like me to put in a word for you, just let me know."

I wasn't sure what he was talking about. Put in a word to who? To Old Jack himself? Nothing else made sense. After all, Mr. Forrester didn't know I wanted to be a Guardsman, and most kids here, if they dreamed at all, dreamed of becoming pirates like Old Jack.

"Thank you, sir," I said, not knowing how else to respond.

He held my gaze for a moment, apparently unsatisfied with my response. "Let me know," he said again, then returned to work.

I walked over toward the cafeteria alone, and in a sour mood. In addition to being puzzled over what Mr. Forrester had been trying to tell me—and disappointed at the prospect that he might be somehow connected to the pirates, I was also irritated that I'd been delayed.

I kept my eyes alert, though, looking for signs of either Mikey or Jamie, who didn't like physics and had elected to take a course in astronavigation instead. We didn't always have a lot of choices on Brighthome, but by our senior year we could at least pick our own classes.

I cut behind the school building, heading between the PX and the gym, hoping to make up for those lost minutes and catch up to Mikey before she got to the cafeteria and took a seat. I found her, too, but not quite the way I'd expected.

As I came around the corner of the PX, an old, ugly, brick building with no windows at all on the ground floor, I saw a couple embracing against the wall ahead of me. At least, that's what it looked like at first.

My momentum carried me forward a couple of steps, my boots rasping softly on the rocks of the path. The guy swivelled his head to glare at me and I saw two things that hit me like a blow to the chest: one, the guy was Burles, without his cronies for a change; and, two, the girl was Mikey.

"Go on, Jenkins," Burles snarled at me. "This is no concern of yours."

When he turned toward me, I could see how he had pinned Mikey to the wall, one large, meaty hand resting solidly on her hip. She was struggling, but Burles ran two meters tall, and nearly an eighth of a ton, and he was solid muscle. I'd seen him working out in the gym, and had long ago decided never to cross him.

But that was Mikey he was holding like that.

Her eyes met mine. I could see no fear in her, just a fury that blazed brighter than the bruise forming on her left cheek. Inside me, I felt a rage of my own kindle.

"Let her go, Burles," I said. My knees were shaking but at least my voice came out steady.

His eyes widened in surprise, then something like an evil grin touched his lips. "You going to make me?" he taunted. His grin grew, and I saw him shift his grip on her, raising his hand and placing it higher on her body.

"Burles—"

"You just blew it, Jenkins. Me and her, we was going to have a nice little time, but now you've made me mad. Maybe now it won't be so nice, you know what I mean?"

Suddenly he grabbed her, spun her around, and pulled her to him. She was between us, facing me. He was behind her, also facing me, and his right hand had crept up to her throat.

"Burles—" I said again, but that was as far as I got.

Something very harsh touched Mikey's face and she went into action. It was too fast for me to follow, but what I thought I saw was her picking up her right foot and slamming it back into Burles' kneecap. I heard a pop. He grunted, and he must have loosened his grip because suddenly she was spinning to face him, her hands moving in a blur.

I don't know how many times she hit him, or where. I saw one blow to his throat and at least three to his body, and I'm sure there were more.

Amazingly, though, it didn't take him out. Oh, he sagged, and ended up going to his knees, but he didn't go down all the way.

Mikey stepped back, panting, out of his reach. I stepped forward to stand beside her, speechless.

Burles, however, had quite a bit to say.

He massaged his throat, glaring daggers at both of us for about a minute. Then he said, "You're dead. Tonight, tomorrow night, it doesn't matter. I'm coming after you, and no teacher, no Prefect, no one is going to save you.

"You're dead. Both of you."

Mikey just looked at him, her face set and hard. I waited for her to say something, anything, but she didn't, and after another moment or two she turned and walked off.

I gave Burles one more glance, still unable to accept what had just happened. To be honest, I was afraid—God, was I afraid—but I was glad, too.

Then I turned and headed after Mikey.

Chapter Four

"Nice place you've got here." Mikey wasn't eating. She made a show of pushing a few things around on her plate, but that was about it.

I wanted to say something, anything, that would comfort her, but I couldn't think of anything. I mean, "Hey, it wasn't you. That sort of thing happens a lot around here," wasn't likely to cheer her up any. So I just kept silent, trying to be supportive, my own food untouched as well.

"Who was that guy, anyway?" I'd been wondering how long it would take her to ask. Apparently, her anger was slower to drain away than my own. Which was, I had to admit, understandable.

"His name is Burles." I sighed, looking out toward the grey landscape beyond the windows, trying to find words to express what I'd gotten used to taking for granted. "There used to be a rumor—still is, I guess, but I don't listen to it anymore—goes back to a time before me, that the pirates sometimes take kids from here. Sort of like a recruitment center, I guess. It makes sense, sort of. I mean, the kids that get sent here are usually the kind most likely to become pirates, aren't they? Some of them, anyway. I never much believed that rumor. Always figured it was just wishful thinking. After all, the pirates could probably do a lot better than a bunch of juvenile delinquents like most of the ones around here.

"But then there are guys like Burles. Every once in a while, someone like him comes through here, and I can see where the pirates might be interested. He's big, he's tough, and he really just doesn't care about things like laws or rules or other people.

"In other words, a perfect pirate."

She frowned. "And I've just made him a sworn enemy."

I nodded. "For both of us."

She looked startled at that, as though she'd forgotten that he'd included me in his threats.

"I'm sorry, Tom," she said.

I smiled, and reached out to touch her hand. "I'm not. I'd rather get the daylights beat out of me anytime than have you suffer what he was going to do to you."

She didn't smile back, but she didn't pull her hand away, either. "But he didn't say he was just going to 'beat the daylights' out of us. He said he was going to kill us. Do you believe him?"

I didn't want to answer that, and I didn't want to meet her gaze any longer, either, but it seemed I had no choice. She refused to let me look away until I said, "Yeah, Mikey. I believe him."

She nodded, then. "So do I, Tom. Unfortunately, I believe he'll try."

I noticed the way she'd phrased that, but before I could say anything she nodded to someone behind me and said, "Who's that?"

I turned and looked and saw Fritz Laramie sitting off by himself. His head was down, but I could see the livid bruise high up on his left cheek. His shoulders were hunched, his body language clearly telling people to leave him alone, and everyone was. But then Burles wasn't there.

I sighed and told Mikey what I'd seen at the rec area the day before. She heard me out without interrupting, but I could tell by her frown that she had some questions.

"I don't understand," she said when I had finished. "Why do you people let him get away with this? Why don't you stand up to him?"

"It's not that simple," I said. "Guys like Fritz over there are loners. They're not used to working with others."

She glared at me. "And it's always easier to stand back and let things happen as long as they're happening to someone else, isn't it?"

I nodded.

"The problem is," she said, "that when it does happen to you, there's no one left to help out."

I opened my mouth to protest but I never got the chance. She stood up, pushing her plate aside, and headed over to Fritz. Shaking my head, I rose and followed.

"Go away," he said when we got close to him.

"All right," Mikey said, "but I want to say something first. I want to tell you that you don't have to face Burles alone. We'll help you if you'll let us. Fight him, Fritz. Don't join with him. That's all."

He looked up, and I could see that he was trying hard not to cry.

"Go away," he said again. "Please, just go away."

Mikey looked at him for a moment, then nodded and walked away. I looked at him, too, but there was absolutely nothing I could say.

Silently, I headed after Mikey.

Chapter Five

"Mikey, wait up!" I called. She didn't stop, but she slowed slightly, and I caught up with her just outside the cafeteria door. "Where are you going?"

She didn't say anything, just pointed toward the building that housed the Administrator's office.

I shook my head. "Mikey, you can't. Mr. Pierson doesn't even *like* us kids." Well, I didn't know that for a fact, but that's what everyone said, and in the four years I'd been on Brighthome I hadn't seen anything to make me think that everyone was wrong. "You can't just walk in on him."

"Watch me," she said, and speeded up again.

I paused, watching her retreating back, and shook my head. But I couldn't help grinning as I did so. She had courage, I had to admit. As well as class.

I glanced back at the cafeteria, but I never really considered going back inside. I didn't think I could be much help to her, but if Mikey was going to see the Administrator, so was I.

Still grinning, I took off after her.

I'd been inside the Administrator's office just once, when I first arrived. He'd glanced at my file, looked at me, and said, "You're in Dorm B. Stay out of trouble." And that was all.

Mr. Pierson's office was at the very top of the building we called the mall. It was mostly administrative offices, but it also had a barber shop, the PX, and a few other little shops, including one that made a pretty decent chocolate malt. And the library was there, one of the three places I spent most of my time. Mr. Pierson had a nicely appointed office, with an outer waiting room and a receptionist—two things that made absolutely no sense to me since he never saw anybody.

Mikey didn't even slow down. She walked right past Clark, the student who worked part-time as the receptionist. I threw Clark an apologetic look, shrugged, and followed her.

Mr. Pierson was behind his desk when we walked in, a sleek, ultra-modern, and very expensive looking thing. He wasn't working, though. He was standing with his back to his desk, looking out the window at the school grounds. The Administrator was a young man, probably in his mid-thirties, with his brown hair just starting to get a bit thin at the top. He was not very big, but he had a certain wiry toughness and an air of meanness that made me think of a snake. Though he didn't turn to look at us, the lines of tension in his body made it clear he knew we were there.

"Is there a problem?" he asked. He said it softly, but the displeasure was plain in his voice.

"Your students are out of hand, Mr. Pierson," Mikey said.

He stiffened but continued to look out the window. "Really?" His voice had gotten even softer and more menacing.

She didn't back down. "Really. There was an attempted rape earlier today, and I've seen how some of your students are conducting a virtual reign of terror right here on campus. You've got to do something."

Now he did turn around, his eyes flicking only briefly toward me before dismissing me and settling on her. "Really?" he asked again. "And what would you have me do, Ms. Delacourte? The kids who come here, most of them, are the most violent and incorrigible teens in the galaxy. Should I place them under house arrest the entire time they're here? Should I request additional funding, so that I can hire guards to monitor every movement by every student? Or should I put up security cameras in every dormitory—" his eyes flicked back to me "—or every cave, so that there is no privacy among the students?"

I'd kept my gaze on Mr. Pierson, but I could feel Mikey getting mad beside me.

"No," she said, "but you should make sure that those kids who want to improve themselves are given the chance to do so in a safe environment."

He laughed. "Improve themselves? Ms. Delacourte, these kids are sent here precisely because they have no wish to improve themselves."

"But—"

He held up a hand, cutting her off. "As for the other half of your statement, perhaps there is something we can do. Your father is a Senator on Markus

Colony, is he not? Perhaps if you could persuade him to make a small contribution to our security funds here, then I—"

That's as far as he got. Mikey spun on her heel and left.

Mr. Pierson didn't say anything else. He just looked at me, an amused smile on his face, and then turned back to the window.

It was all too sudden for me. I hesitated for a moment before leaving, and by the time I got outside Mikey was nowhere in sight. I knew she was mad, but I wasn't sure why. This was Brighthome, after all. What had she expected? I just hoped she wasn't mad at—or disappointed in—me.

I sighed, but decided not to follow her. If she'd wanted company, she'd have waited for me in the hallway. Besides, as long as I was here, there was something else I wanted to do.

"Hello, Mr. Murphy," I said as I walked past his station. Mr. Murphy was Brighthome's librarian, and the closest thing I had to a friend among the staff.

"Hi, Tom," he said. "It's open. As usual." He grinned as he added that last part, but it was a sad sort of smile. Not many students ever came into the library, and most of those who did just occasionally checked the newsservs for reports of the latest pirate activity.

There were actual books in this library, several thousand volumes that were mostly fiction. I'd checked a lot of them out, reading them in the cave while Jamie played his vid games or late at night when the dream was keeping me from sleep. But usually when I came to the library it wasn't to check

out a book. No, usually when I came to the library
it was to continue my search.

"Good luck, Tom," Mr. Murphy said as I signed
in. "Maybe this'll be the day."

I nodded and headed back toward the workstation.

The station itself was in a small cubicle set back
in one corner of the library. There was a comfortable chair and a standard keyboard and display unit.
The difference was that this station was the only
means we had to connect to the larger newsservs
and databases. The display units in our desks and
dorms could only access what the administration
wanted us to see: educational programs and a highly
selective and limited range of news stories. This
station, though, could access everything, and so its
usage was restricted and monitored.

Which was fine with me. I didn't want to do anything subversive. I just wanted to find out who I
was.

Years ago, when I first came to Brighthome and
after the initial shock had worn off, I started searching for any mention of people disappearing. Mr.
Murphy had been a big help to me, teaching me
how to use the station, devising various search strat-
egies, and showing me how to interpret the results.

I'd started with a request for the names of all
the people who had vanished at around the time
I'd been found. I defined that as people who had
moved without leaving a forwarding address as well
as ships that had disappeared without a trace. That
didn't work, though. The search came back with
a list that was too long for the machine's memory,
and far too many names for me to ever check out.
So I narrowed my search. I started with the system

closest to where I'd been found, searching for names of people who'd disappeared and then asking for more and more information about them until I could rule them out. Some didn't have kids. Others had disappeared in natural disasters of one sort or another and were presumed dead. All of them, eventually, were crossed off my list, and then I'd go on to the next system, expanding outward in an ever-widening spiral.

My search was made more difficult by the fact that our equipment was not exactly cutting edge, as Mr. Murphy was fond of pointing out, and by the fact that access to this workstation was limited. Each student could only use it for half an hour each week, and even though Jamie had signed over his time to me that just wasn't long enough.

But maybe it was long enough to find out who I wasn't.

In the nearly four years I'd been doing this, I'd worked my way through a couple of dozen systems, and had found no one who could have been my family. Realistically, the first dozen systems had been my best bet. Passenger ships tended to travel set routes. It was unlikely that one would have come in from farther away than one of those first ten or twelve systems I'd checked. I was still looking, still broadening my search, but I was no longer confident I'd find my family.

And that was good. In my mind, I'd built up a picture of who they'd been. The way I saw it, my parents were both Guardsmen and one of them—or maybe both—had been assigned to deal with the pirates. Whichever one it was had done too good a job, however, and the pirates laid a trap for them. In my mind, and in my heart, my parents had been captured by the pirates, and my own memories had been suppressed. Naturally, since they were Guardsmen, there would be no record of them in the public data banks. Which meant that, by not finding my family this way, I was really that much closer to finding out who I really was.

I was just about done with this latest system, only two more disappearances on my list. Mr. Murphy came back as I keyed in the request for additional information, and I saw his shoulders tense as we both waited for the response.

It didn't take long. The tension went out of him as the information came back: one "disappearance" was a man who was probably skipping out on child support; the other was a family whose ship disappeared in space, but both their children were girls.

"I'm sorry, Tom," Mr. Murphy said.

"Thanks," I said, shutting down the workstation and standing up. "For everything."

He nodded and I headed toward the door. If he noticed that I didn't seem too terribly upset by the results, he didn't say anything about it.

Chapter Six

"So where've you been?"

I knew it was Jamie even before he spoke. I'd heard him come in and flop on his bunk beneath me. "How'd you know I was here?" I asked.

I could hear the humor in his voice as he said, "C'mon, Tom. I've slept in this bunk for two years, now. I can tell if you're in yours or not." He reached up and gave my sagging mattress a playful poke. "So, where've you been?"

It was midafternoon. I still hadn't seen Mikey and I was worrying about her. Not that I thought Burles was going to do anything right away. For one thing, I had the impression she'd busted up his knee pretty good. For another, he was the kind of guy who liked to make you sweat before he came after you. He was good at that. Still, I was worried about Mikey, even though she'd already shown she could take care of herself. Burles might be the worst of the

Brighthome baddies, but he was far from the only one. And she was probably still mad enough to do something foolish.

"I've been napping," I said, which wasn't true. I'd been trying to sleep. I certainly needed a nap, but thoughts of Mikey kept getting in the way. "Before that, I was at the library for a while."

"Oh? How'd it go?"

I shrugged. "The same as always," I said.

"Oh. I'm sorry, Tom," he said, and for once his voice was serious.

I shrugged again.

He was silent for a moment, then, "I heard what happened. With Burles, I mean. You need any help?"

That was Jamie. A little guy, and about as well-built as a wet noodle, but I knew his offer was serious. His loyalty came hard, but once you'd earned it, he'd do anything for you.

"Thanks, buddy," I said, "but I don't think there's any help for us. I'm just going to try to stay out of his way until he turns eighteen and gets kicked out of here."

Brighthome wasn't that big of a place. Half a dozen dormitories—four for boys, two for girls, three classroom buildings, a cafeteria, a gymnasium, an infirmary, and the mall. And the spaceport, or what passed for one here: three landing pads, one large, old hangar, and half a dozen broken down old shuttles for us to use.

Not a lot of places to hide.

Jamie punched my mattress again. "Good luck," he said. Then, in a more serious tone, he added, "And be careful."

What could I say to that?

CHAPTER SEVEN

Jamie and I always ate an early dinner. On those evenings when we could get out of the structured leisure activities, it gave us more time to spend in the caves. It also kept us away from Burles and his crowd, who tended to eat later.

There were half a dozen other kids spread out among the tables. Fritz Laramie was one of them, eating by himself at a table near the back door. Our eyes met for a moment, but then he dropped his gaze to his food, a clear sign that he didn't want any company.

"Just a minute," I said to Jamie, and went over to him anyway.

He didn't look up.

"Look, Fritz," I said, "I know this isn't easy, but I want you to know that you don't have to handle it alone. What Mikey said to you earlier is true. You've got friends if you want them."

He still didn't say anything, and after a moment I went and got myself a plate of food and joined Jamie at a different table.

"What was that all about?" he asked.

"Trouble," I said. "More than he can handle, I'm afraid."

I looked over at Jamie and saw a very serious expression on his face. "More than any of us can handle, I think."

"You've heard, huh?" I asked.

"Word gets around, Tom. You know that."

I nodded. "What did you hear?"

"That he's been marked." He glanced down at his plate, then back up to me. "Stay out of it, Tom. Don't get involved."

I shook my head. "That's one of the rules around here, isn't it, Jamie? Don't get involved. Well, I'm getting a little tired of that rule."

There wasn't much to say to that, I guess. He started eating, and so did I. As I did so, though, I couldn't help watching Fritz, and noticing the way he kept one eye on the front door at all times. If Burles walked in, I knew that Fritz would be out the back door in a minute, and I couldn't help feeling sorry for him.

"Don't get involved," I said softly. "Yep, I'm definitely getting tired of that rule."

We were still eating in silence several minutes later when Mikey came up to our table and took a seat next to me. She had a plate with her, and I was amazed to see how high she'd heaped it with various kinds of food.

"You're going to eat all that?" I asked.

She smiled at me. Across from me, I saw Jamie stiffen slightly, but I didn't know why.

"Hey," she said, "I told you some of what I've done these past few years. Believe me, this food may not seem like much to you, but compared to some of what I've eaten, this stuff is fit for a king."

I smiled and remembered my manners. "Jamie," I said, turning to look at him, "this is Mikey. Mikey, Jamie, my best friend."

The two of them looked at each other for a moment as though they were prizefighters sizing up an opponent. Jamie I could understand. He was naturally slow to warm up to people—though once he did, he was a fierce friend—but Mikey I wasn't so sure about.

She stuck out her hand, then, and everything was fine. Or so I thought.

"Pleased to meet you," she said.

Jamie took her hand, but only briefly, and he didn't say anything in return. Instead, he stood up, leaving half his food untouched, and gave me a significant look.

"I've got things to do, Tom. I'll meet you later—you know where." And with that he was gone.

His departure was stiff and sudden and left an uncomfortable tension behind. Mikey gave me a look as if to say, "What's *his* problem?" and then shrugged, picked up her fork, and started to eat.

I grinned. I couldn't help it. Seeing somebody actually enjoy Brighthome cooking was such a rare sight that it helped me to forget about Jamie's strange behavior. Besides, I figured he'd explain it to me later, when we met at the cave.

I picked up my own fork and turned my attention back to my plate. I was practically finished anyway, and it didn't take long for me to push it away, empty. Wiping my mouth with the little paper napkins they provided, I glanced over at Mikey and almost dropped my napkin. Her plate was nearly empty, and at the rate she was shoveling it, she'd be done in no time.

"Gee, Mikey," I said. "You eat like a Guardsman." I'd seen a vid on them a week or so ago. In it, I'd heard that Guardsmen always eat fast because, just like firemen, they have no idea when the alarm might sound, and they want to make sure they get everything eaten.

She looked up, startled, and then grinned weakly. "Nah, Tom. Not that. It comes from eating on the run. I could never stay in one place for long, so I had to learn to do everything fast."

I nodded. "I can see that."

She went back to her food, but I noticed she was eating more slowly now. Even so, it was only a couple of minutes before she pushed her plate away, clean as a whistle and utterly empty.

"Now what?" she asked.

I shrugged. "Now I go and meet Jamie and find out what's bugging him."

She didn't say anything, just held my gaze, a slight smile tugging at her lips. I waited, but she still didn't say anything, and eventually I was forced to add, "You want to come along?"

Her smile erupted at my words, and I was suddenly glad I'd asked her.

"Sure," she said. "Where?"

"You'll see," I said.

Rising, I grabbed Jamie's plate along with my own, headed over to the return counter, and then led her out into the early evening.

Chapter Eight

We were walking along the rock-lined path that led over toward the hills. That path turned away before the edge of the campus, angling off in the direction of the girls' dorms. I'd always wondered why they even bothered with paths, here. It wasn't like there was any grass to kill or anything. The scenery was all bare, grey dust and rock, all except for these little white paths. Maybe it was just to keep our boots a little cleaner.

It wasn't dark yet, though green Antillus was up over the hills already, and the evening softened everything around us. There were no sounds, no scents, and once again I started thinking about what evening might be like on my homeworld. Were there nightbirds, whose gentle songs filled the air, I wondered, or predators whose cries rent the deepening gloom? Or was I born on one of the colonies, as bleak and barren as Brighthome beyond their sealed domes, where evening was just another hour on the clock?

This time of day always filled me with melancholy, as the sunset bloomed overhead and I found myself wondering what palette painted the sky back home. This was the time, more so even than the night, when I felt the loss of my family and my memory most strongly.

Mikey wasn't helping my mood, either. She was as silent as I, and after a while it occurred to me that she seemed distracted. Here I was, all caught up in my own troubles, and for all I knew her own were ten times worse.

I reached out and touched her hand. "Are you all right?" I asked. "Burles didn't—"

"No," she said quickly. "Nothing like that. I was just thinking about Mr. Pierson, and about how mad that whole thing makes me."

"I know," I said, "but what can we do?"

She glared at me. "I don't know, Tom, but somebody ought to do something."

I didn't know what to say to that so I merely nodded.

We walked a bit farther and then she said, "I'm sorry. It's not your fault. I just . . ." She ran out of words at that point, but I got the picture.

"I know," I said. "Me, too."

We walked some more, each of us caught up in our own thoughts.

"So," she said, a few minutes later, "I hear you're a pilot." Her voice was brighter, more upbeat, and if her conversation seemed a bit forced, it was still better than her earlier strained silence.

I grinned, but kept my face turned away so she couldn't see it. "You hear a lot," I said.

"The others talk a lot, you know. I listen. It's something you get good at on the streets."

I nodded. "Yeah, I'm a pilot, though only of the reconditioned runabouts they call ships, here. It's not like I could fly a pirate gunboat or anything. Why? I mean, why bring it up?"

She shrugged again. "Oh, I don't know. I guess I thought maybe we could go flying sometime. I like space."

"Sure," I said. "In fact, tomorrow's Saturday; Jamie and I always try to sneak off for a few hours on the weekend. When Mr. Forrester hasn't grounded me for daydreaming, that is," I added. "Would you like to come along?"

"I'd love to," she said. "But will Jamie mind?"

"Nah," I said, trying to downplay the scene at the cafeteria. "He's not normally like that. You'll see."

Which seemed to exhaust our store of conversation for the moment. We finished our walk in silence, but it was a comfortable, companionable silence.

Outwardly, I kept my face impassive, but inwardly I was smiling.

Chapter Nine

"This is it, huh?"

The cave mouth yawned before us like a big black hole in the side of the hill. I'd gone inside hundreds of times and it still looked a little spooky to me. I could just imagine how it seemed to Mikey. Somehow, though, I wasn't surprised that she didn't act all that scared.

"This is it," I answered her. "Don't worry, we've got some lanterns stashed. Come on. I'll show you."

Two paces inside and it was pitch black. Funny, I never felt claustrophobic here, even at those times in my life when the dream was occurring most often. It was like, because I knew this place, because I knew the size of the room around me, I didn't have to worry, even though I couldn't see it.

"Straight ahead," I said, "two more steps. Duck here, there's a stalactite hanging down. Okay, now stop. On your right is a boulder. Feel it?"

She was right behind me. I could hear her breathing. I could even feel her warmth—or at least I thought I could. But I couldn't see her.

"Yes." Her voice came out of the dark, bodiless and eerie.

"Good. Now, slowly move your hand down behind it. You should find several lamps."

I could have picked one up first and showed her, but I wanted her to be able to find them in the dark. In the years I'd been at Brighthome, I'd shown four other people the way into the cave, and I'd learned that this was the best method.

A sudden glow appeared beside me, lighting up her face like a smile. I grinned myself, picked up a lantern of my own, and gestured at our surroundings.

It was a large room, about the size of two of our cafeteria's tables, or big enough to hold a couple dozen people. The floor was sand, with five or six good-sized rocks strewn about at random. There was only the one stonecicle hanging down, and I'd often wondered at the irony of it being right in the way like that.

"Pretty nice," she said.

"Oh, you haven't seen anything yet. This is just the outer room."

She glanced over at me but I didn't say anything more, just led off toward the back wall. As we came closer, it became apparent that the wall, which looked solid from more than two feet away, had shifted at some point. It was cracked down the middle, and the portion on the right jutted forward a little ways, creating a little corridor that disappeared into the hill.

"In there?" she asked.

"In there," I said. I hung back, letting her take the lead if she wanted, but she motioned for me to proceed.

There was a glittering of color running along the wall to our left, a pretty mixture of red and blue ores combined with some colorless crystals that caught our lantern light and threw it back at us.

"Wow," she said, taking it all in. "This is really neat."

"Thanks," I said, as though I were responsible for it all. And I guess I was, in a way, at least for showing it to her.

The corridor went back about fifteen feet, twisting and turning all the way. It also started to narrow after the first five feet or so, and by the end the rock was brushing against us on both sides.

"How much farther?" she asked.

"Almost there."

We had to crawl the last little ways, and the final obstacle was an outjutting of stone that hung down from the ceiling. Not a real stalactite, more a harder, denser layer that hadn't eroded as fast as the surrounding rock. I had to lie flat on my back and sort of inch my way forward, and even at that I could feel it pressing hard against my chest.

I was puffing slightly when I finally wriggled free and turned to shine my light for Mikey. This was about the only time I ever envied Jamie his size. It was always a struggle for me to get past this point, but he just popped right through with no trouble at all.

Mikey was slightly smaller than me, and I hadn't expected her to have any trouble with this part at all. I was wrong. She made it, eventually, after trying two or three different approaches, but her face was beet red afterward, and I was pretty sure it wasn't all from exertion, either.

I didn't say anything, just held up my light and cast its glow around. "This is our foyer," I said. "The tunnel we just left turns enough that our light can't be seen in that outer room, and the rock surrounding us blocks out most probes. In other words, Mikey, this is the most private place on Brighthome. Welcome to it."

She smiled and nodded. "I can see why the teachers don't know about it. None of them would ever fit through that last spot."

I had to chuckle at that. "Not unless they all went on a diet." Which wasn't a particularly nice thing to say, but it was mostly true. Mostly.

Mikey lifted her own lamp and sent its beam around the foyer. It wasn't as big as the outer chamber—"The Doorstep," as we sometimes called it— but it was pretty large. Roughly circular, it had a diameter of some fifteen feet, and the broken stalagmite in the very center of the room looked like a little coffee table or something.

The walls glittered with crystals and a reemergence of the red and blue veins we'd seen in the tunnel. In addition, there were two corridors leading off, one to the right, and one in the back wall. They led into a maze of tunnels beyond, some of them hooking up with others, some of them doubling back on themselves, others leading nowhere. Jamie and I had explored most of them, but not even we knew all their twists and turns.

"Come on," I said. "Let's go meet Jamie," and I headed off to the right.

There was another room beyond, with a large column in the middle made by a stalagmite and stalactite that had finally joined after who knew how many thousands of years. One of the side walls was a fairy curtain of mini-stalactites colored through with red, blue, and green minerals.

Mikey stopped in this room, looking around. "You know," she said after a few minutes, "this doesn't make a lot of sense. What could have caused this, I wonder? After all, this is a moon, not a planet. There is no free-flowing water to have carved something like this, or to drip down over the eons and form the stalactites and stalagmites."

I shrugged. "'There are more things in heaven and earth, Horatio . . . '"

She surprised me by completing the quote, "'than are dreamt of in your philosophy.' So what's your point?"

I shrugged again. It seemed I was doing a lot of that around her. "Simply that we can't always explain everything. I mean, maybe this moon was once a part of a planet; or maybe there's another explanation for how all this stuff formed. The point is, I don't know, can't know, but just because I can't explain it doesn't mean it isn't pretty."

She looked at me with an unfathomable expression on her face and I realized that I was probably overreacting. All she said, though, was, "You're right, Tom, and I'm sorry if I implied otherwise. The galaxy *is* a strange and wondrous place—at least at times—and we should enjoy it. But that doesn't mean we shouldn't try to figure things out, does it? After all, these caves wouldn't be any less pretty if you *could* explain them, would they?"

I shook my head, at a loss for what else to say. I wasn't used to being taken to task like that. The funny thing was, I would have expected it to make me angry, but all I felt was slightly embarrassed.

There was only one opening in this room other than the one we came through. I gestured toward it with my lamp and then headed for it, hoping she would take the hint.

She did, and followed me without another word.

Chapter Ten

Our campsite was in the neatest room we'd found. The far wall was another one of those stone curtains, but this one was shot through with a brilliant red crystalline ore that turned it into a firefall in our lamplight. There were several dozen stalactites hanging down, but all of them were too small to pose a problem, and no stalagmites sticking up—except for one monster over by the far wall that had risen in something of a Christmas tree shape.

There were crystals in all the rocks: overhead, in the walls, underfoot, and at least half a dozen veins of various colors running through the rock. Mikey took one look and gasped. I shared her pleasure, even though I'd seen this room countless times before.

The only sour spot was Jamie. He lay on his bedroll, playing one of his vid games, resentment smoldering on his face. He didn't even look up when we came in, although he had to have heard us talking in the other room. For the first time in a long while, I felt myself growing annoyed with him.

"Hey, buddy," I said, trying to keep the irritation out of my voice, "how's it going?"

He glanced up, shrugged, and went back to his game.

I frowned and looked over at Mikey to see how she was taking all this, but she was still looking around at the walls. Or pretending to, at least.

In the silence that followed, I heard a sudden ping and a sigh and knew that Jamie's game was over at last. Turning to him, ready to extend an olive branch and see if we could put all this unpleasantness behind us, I was surprised to see him rising to his feet and dusting himself off.

"Long day," he said, his face stiff and impassive. "Think I'll head back to the dorm and turn in. Good night."

"Jamie—"

He turned his closed up face in my direction and the pain I saw in his eyes stopped me from saying anything more. What was he feeling? I wondered. And why was he feeling it?

I could only nod, my hand half-raised in his direction, as though I'd been stopped halfway through throwing him a lifeline, and in a way that's just how I felt.

"Maybe we can talk later," I said.

He nodded, and for a moment I thought his mask was going to crack, but then it closed up again and he walked out of the room.

"Tom?" Mikey's voice sounded much louder in the silence of his departure.

"Yes?"

"Why doesn't he like me?"

"I don't know, Mikey. I honestly don't know."

She nodded at that, and started walking slowly around the room, shining her light on the walls and examining the various colors and crystals. I unrolled my sleeping bag, sat down on it, and watched her.

There was a tension about her that at first I passed off as annoyance with Jamie, but it eventually occurred to me that it may have been caused by something else: me.

We'd been alone together before, that first night talking in the light of Antillus and the walk out along the path, to name just a couple, but this was the first time things had felt awkward between us. Thinking about it, I realized that it was probably because we were in my territory now, the place where I felt most comfortable.

She was probably expecting me to try something, I thought, and I couldn't help wondering how she would react if I did.

"Mikey," I said.

She stiffened and slowly turned around to face me, crossing her arms across her chest and leaning back against the wall. "Yes?"

I didn't have to be an expert at reading body language to know that my question had just been answered. "Can you think of anything we can do to help Fritz? I saw him at dinner earlier and he looked scared."

She smiled softly, and it may have been my imagination but I thought I saw a hint of sadness in her eyes as she said, "I don't think so, Tom. The next move is up to him. We can help him, but only if he wants us to."

I nodded at that. "That's what I thought. Well, let's hope he wants us to."

We lapsed back into silence, but this time it was more comfortable. She went back to studying the walls, and I went back to watching her.

Sometime later, feeling all gentlemanly and mature, I walked her back to her dorm and watched her go inside. It had been an enjoyable evening, even with Jamie's inexplicable behavior, but I felt oddly disappointed as I walked back home, thinking of Mikey every step of the way.

Chapter Eleven

I slipped into our room as quietly as I could. I doubted Jamie would be asleep yet—after living with the guy for a couple of years, I knew his habits pretty well—but I didn't want to take anything for granted.

Preparing for bed didn't take long. Within five minutes I was in my bunk. I heard his breathing change as I climbed up the ladder, and knew he was awake.

"So, buddy," I said softly after getting myself comfortable, "you want to talk about it, or you want to go around being mad at me for no reason?"

"No reason!" I was startled by the anger I heard in his voice. "You brought her to our cave, Tom! That's *our* place, man!"

I sighed. I could have corrected him on that. It was *my* place. I found it before he even came to Brighthome. I'd chosen to share it with him; and now I was choosing to share it with Mikey.

I could have said all that. It was perfectly true, but he knew it already. Besides, I could hear the pain in his voice that lay under his anger. I just couldn't figure out where it came from.

"It's still our place," I said. "Jamie, you're my best friend. Nothing has changed that. Heck, nothing *could* change that, and you know it. So what's the deal?"

I heard his breathing slow. If I didn't know better, I'd have said that he was trying hard not to cry. The thing was, Jamie didn't do that. I'd seen him beaten up by bigger kids; I'd seen him staring off into the blackness of space, loneliness written all over his face; but, in the two years or so I'd known him, I had never seen him cry.

"Look," I said, "you remember what it was like when you first came here. Not knowing anyone. Not having any friends. It was rough. Well, I remember it, too, and I'm just trying to be a friend to her. That's all. You've got to understand that, Jamie."

And that was as much as I could say. If he couldn't see that she wasn't a threat to him, well, then he wouldn't believe me if I told him. But he would see it, eventually.

"Do you think she's pretty?" he asked after a moment.

I wasn't sure just what to make of that. "She's all right, I guess," I said.

"Aw, come on, Tom," he said, poking my mattress. "I've seen how you look at her. She's pretty, isn't she?" There was a playful note in his voice, and if it sounded a bit forced, so what? I'd take that over what I'd heard earlier, any day. Still, I was glad for the darkness, if only so he couldn't see me blush.

"Yeah, Jamie," I said reluctantly. "She's pretty."

He chuckled, and right at that moment I couldn't think of a sound I'd rather hear.

The silence stretched out for a while, but it wasn't strained like it had been. When he spoke again, a few minutes later, his voice was back to normal.

"She coming along tomorrow?" he asked.

"You mean the shuttle trip? Yes. But if you'd like, we can spend the rest of the day together."

"Just you and me?" he asked.

"Just you and me," I said. "All right?"

He sighed. "All right. But, Tom?"

"Yeah?"

"Keep your mind on your flying, okay?"

"You got it, buddy," I said.

He poked my mattress one more time and then we drifted off to sleep.

Chapter Twelve

Brighthome has many sides. It looks one way when you're staring out the window in one of Mr. Forrester's astronomy classes; it looks completely different when you're sitting up in the hills at night, watching Antillus rise; and it looks still different in the grey light of morning.

Of all the views I'd seen of Brighthome, the one I liked best was the one I was seeing now: the sight of it receding in my viewer.

The shuttle was old. It was a reconditioned Space Guard runabout, and I'd have bet a tour of our caves that it was older than I was. It had the marks of a long life, scars both inside and out that told of countless refits, but I loved it. Once a week, if my behavior in class didn't get me in trouble, I got to take this shuttle off the rock I lived on and spend a few hours totally free. It could have been an old pirate vessel and I'd still have loved it.

"Hey, this isn't bad," Mikey said, from the seat to my right. She was navigator this trip. Normally, that was Jamie's role, but he'd relinquished it to her. I hadn't been able to figure out why, either: whether he was trying to make up for the way he'd treated her earlier or if he wanted her to have to prove herself. He could be like that.

Jamie was seated behind her, watching her carefully. She didn't seem to mind the scrutiny. In fact, in the thirty minutes or so we'd been aboard—counting twenty minutes of pre-launch checks and ten minutes of actual flight—he hadn't had to correct her once.

I smiled at that.

"Yes," I said. "Probably not up to your standards, of course, but we like her."

I was kidding, but she shot me a sudden suspicious look. "What do you mean?"

I blinked. "Well, you said yourself you were something of a galactic hobo. I figured you'd probably stowed away on the flagship itself at one time."

She relaxed at that, and even chuckled. "A 'galactic hobo,' eh? I like that. Maybe that's what we should call ourselves, what do you think?"

I grinned again and looked at Jamie. "You like that, buddy?"

He smiled, too, and nodded. "Sure. The Galactic Hobos. Why not?"

We cleared Brighthome's atmosphere and I put us into a high, slow orbit, the nose of our craft pointing toward the stars.

"Well, Navigator, where should we go? Antares? Sirius? Or even the far-off world of Earth?" It was my customary question, and I always waited until we were in space to ask it. I got to fly this old bird;

I always let my navigator select our course, and we never set our course on the ground. No one from Brighthome did. Unquestionably, that was the efficient way to do it, but we weren't flying these old buckets for efficiency. We were flying them to get away from Brighthome for a while, and that meant getting off the ground and into space before we even thought about where we were heading.

I glanced over at Jamie as I asked this question. I thought I saw a shadow of an emotion flicker across his face, but he covered it up well. I didn't blame him for being hurt—this was the first time I'd asked that of someone other than him—but I was glad to see he was trying to have fun.

I gave him a wink and a grin and turned my attention to Mikey. She was grinning, too, but her smile was more playful than mine.

"Earth?" she said. "Really? I wouldn't have thought our craft would have such a range."

I nodded and gestured toward the stars. "Indeed, anywhere you care to name. As long as we can get there and back in six hours," I added, nodding toward the indicator on our boards. "After that, the folks on Brighthome get worried and come looking for us."

Her grin widened. "Six hours? Why, then, let us head even farther. Let us set our sights on an entirely new galaxy. We shall become the first *Inter*-Galactic Hobos."

"Sorry," Jamie spoke up, his voice doing a good imitation of genuine sympathy, "Tom and I did that last time, exploring—and plundering—the wonders of Andromeda. Truly a sight to see."

I turned back to my controls, fighting to keep a fresh grin off my face. He'd agreed to have fun, I knew, but that didn't mean he couldn't throw a shot every now and then.

"We're wasting time," I said. "Set a course, Navigator."

She did, and quickly, too, which surprised me. Jamie had been flying with me for over a year— ever since I earned my flames, as a matter of fact— and he knew this ship as well as everyone but the folks who'd built her, and he couldn't have plotted and set a course any faster.

"Was that a random setting?" he asked. "Or do you have an actual destination in mind?"

This time there was a slight edge to his voice, but I couldn't really blame him. He was trying to be nice, mostly, and she was close to showing him up. I guess I should have been happy that it was only a *slight* edge in his voice.

"See for yourself, coach," she said, rising from her seat.

He motioned for her to stay where she was and scanned her settings over her shoulder. Turning to me, he said, "We're slotted for a close fly-by of Antillus, Captain."

I nodded. "How close?"

"Too close. Much too deep inside the gravity well."

I nodded again. "Mikey, did you have any particular reason for choosing that setting, or was it, as Jamie said, simply random?"

She gave me another one of her long, hard stares. "Why?" she countered after a moment.

"Because this ship—like all the shuttles on Brighthome—is designed for the use of some fairly young, and fairly rebellious, juvenile delinquents. There are all sorts of safety lockouts on the computer, and one of them prevents us from falling too far into a strong gravity well. If I try to engage the course you've selected, the computer will give me a warning, and if we don't alter the flight plan it will shut me down completely and fly us home on autopilot."

"Oh." She looked at me some more.

"So, did you have a reason for wanting to fly by Antillus?"

She surprised me by blushing suddenly and looking away. There was a port on her right, and she turned to look out it as she answered in a soft voice, "Actually, Tom, yes, there is a reason. I was looking at Antillus that night we first talked. It seemed kind of lucky for me, I guess, and I wanted a closer look at it. That's all," she added, shrugging.

Behind her, Jamie coughed slightly, and I, too, turned to look out my port.

"Jamie," I said after a moment, "would you mind?"

"You got it, Tom." He rose and headed aft.

"What's he doing?" Mikey turned back to me, her face once more calm and composed.

I had recovered as well and I managed to give her a grin that wasn't too shaky. "Jamie loves computers," I said. "Spends half his time playing with them and the other half taking them apart. At least, it seems that way, sometimes. He's the best vid player on Brighthome—and there are a lot of vid players on Brighthome—and when he finishes a game, he takes it apart to see if there were any tricks he missed. Anyway, he knows an awful lot about computers, and sometimes he can override the lockouts. I asked him to try. We'll know in a few minutes whether you'll get that fly-by or not."

She held my gaze for a moment, her face totally serious. "Tom—" she started.

I didn't know what she was going to say. I didn't even know if I *wanted* to know, but I didn't get a chance to find out. Jamie came back just then and announced, "I think I got it, Captain. Kick her in gear and let's see if you get a warning."

Mikey and I held each other's eyes for another second or two—or maybe longer; it certainly felt longer to me—and then I had to look away. Turning back to my board, I said, "Course laid in. Engaging now," and reached out for the controls.

A gentle push on the stick, eyes raking right to left, left to right, waiting for the warning tone. Nothing happened, except that we slowly turned and started heading toward Antillus.

Chapter Thirteen

I spent the next ten minutes watching my controls and trying to figure out how to ask Mikey where she'd learned to navigate. The course she'd laid in was efficient, and she'd done it so quickly, but I couldn't find an opening to bring it up. And that was one of Brighthome's cardinal lessons, even if it never appeared in a single text book: don't pry.

"So," Mikey said, breaking the silence for us, "would you like an area scan, Captain?"

I laughed. "Of course. And bring the weapons system on line, too. I'll want a full systems report, Navigator."

She turned back to her console, forcing me to add, "Mikey, this is an old runabout. We don't have weapons, and we don't have scanners."

She paused, then swivelled around to face me again, her face completely serious. "Actually, Captain, that's not strictly true. This is an old runabout, true, but it's an old Space Guard runabout. The weapons have been removed, but my console shows the scanning system is still intact."

"What?" That was Jamie, fairly leaping from his seat to peer over her shoulder. "Where?"

She reached over to the console directly between us. It was bare metal, no switches, dials, lights, or buttons; just grey, smooth metal. Our instructors had never mentioned it, and we'd always assumed that the controls—whatever they were—had been removed. Her hand slid across the metal and down the front, disappearing briefly beneath the console. I heard a faint click, and then the entire top of the console slid back, disappearing into the wall.

It was a cover. I just stared and shook my head. Jamie's ears were a little red, I saw, but he didn't look away for a moment.

"Show me," he said. Then, after a moment, he added, "Please," in a softer voice.

I could only give half an ear to her explanations. Most of my attention had to stay focused on my flying. We were in clear space, no rocks or anything in our area, but I'd learned not to take any chances. Not when I had crew at risk as well.

It turned out that all we had were short-range systems: a modified pulse radar for close-in work and a hyperwave detection grid for in-system navigation. Which pretty much meant we could see what was going on in the Antillus system, if anything, but that was it. I chuckled when she said that. A minute ago, we had nothing; short-range systems seemed great to Jamie and me.

The best thing about her explanation, however, was her manner in giving it. She could have lorded it over us: "You guys have been flying this for how

long and never looked at this console?" She didn't.
She was cool and crisp, delivering her instructions
in an efficient and effective manner.

Professional, I thought. *She looks like she's done
this sort of thing before.*

Boy, did I want to ask her about that. Maybe, I
thought, remembering the look she'd given me earlier and the statement she started to make, maybe
a time would come when I could ask her.

"System clear, Captain," she said. "No ships moving in or out." Then, to Jamie, she said, "See, this
screen is the hyperwave detection grid. It takes a
little getting used to, but once you've done that you
can read the entire system at a glance. What it does
is show gravity sources in hyperspace. They appear
as holes; the bigger the hole, the stronger the gravity
well. Movement appears as ripples, but since the
computer has all the moons and planets already in
its memory banks, it's able to cancel them out. That
way, any time you see ripples on the screen you
know there's a ship—or at least an unidentified
gravity source—moving out there. Now, look. With
this I can lay a schematic of the Antillus system
directly over the screen. We'll do that for now to
help you visualize it all. Here's the sun, that large
hole near the top of the screen. This dot is
Brighthome; this larger one is Antillus. We're this
blue cross about halfway between the two. We can
change scale, and we can shift focus to other parts
of the system, too."

Behind her, Jamie grunted as though he already
knew all that, but I noticed he was taking in every
word.

I just grinned and kept on flying.

Chapter Fourteen

Mikey had laid in a slow, fuel-efficient course, and I saw no reason to speed things up. She was involved in checking Jamie out on the scanners and I was in no hurry. She'd taken him on a guided tour of the entire system, and was only now bringing him back to our immediate area.

"Close orbit in ten minutes," I said, just to update them.

They were still on the hyperwave detector, but now Jamie was at the controls. There was no seat at these controls—they were positioned for access by either the pilot or the navigator—but he had just enough room to stand between us. I could see the ghostly shapes swimming on his screen, and longed for the opportunity to spend some time with them. Soon enough, I thought, orbit would be established. I could put the controls on automatic then and do some playing myself.

"What's that?" Jamie asked.

"Antillus," Mikey replied. Again, I was surprised at the patience I heard in her voice, even though she'd already pointed the planet out to him.

"No, I mean that." He adjusted the scale, enlarging the images on the screen, and pointed to a small gravity source very close to the planet. Even at full magnification, it was barely a dot.

"You've got good eyes," she complimented him, "and an even better question. I don't know what that is." The patience was gone from her voice, replaced by puzzlement. "It looks like a space station, but it's in an awfully low orbit. Besides, I didn't think there were any stations around Antillus."

"There aren't," I spoke up, just to keep my hand in the conversation. "None anyone on Brighthome has ever mentioned, anyway."

Jamie looked over at me and said, "There's only one way to find out, Captain."

I nodded. "Good point. Navigator?"

Mikey manipulated some controls quickly. "New course plotted and laid in, sir."

I had to smile at that. She was really good. And I kind of liked hearing her call me "sir."

I engaged the new course, eyes raking across my own screens. We would approach it from the front of its orbit, which meant she'd not only laid in a fast course, she'd also laid in an efficient one. "Intercept in twelve minutes," I said. The station—if that's what it was—was partway around the planet from us. Without the hyperwave, we would never have spotted it.

"A station around Antillus," Jamie said softly. "I wonder what it is?"

My only answer was to nudge the throttle forward a little. We'd know soon enough.

Chapter Fifteen

It was an ugly thing, that was for sure, kind of like a short, fat stick with donuts on each end. Docking rings, I assumed, with living quarters and the operational area located in the central corridor.

The place was dark. No sign of ships or other activity. And it felt *old*.

"Guesses?" I asked. "Anybody?"

No one answered.

"Comments? Suggestions?"

After a moment, Jamie said, "Depends on how much adventure we're all up for," and he glanced over at Mikey, as if assessing her. Or daring her. "We could just go up and dock. We've got suits, though we'll undoubtedly be in trouble when we get back."

I nodded. EVA's were strictly forbidden—except in the case of an actual emergency, of course. Frank, the guy who maintained all six shuttles on Brighthome—would be sure and check the air supply on the suits. He'd know right away that we'd gone out, and even though he was a friend, he'd have to report us. We'd lose our shuttle privileges for a month, probably.

"That's one option," I said. "You said, 'Depends.' I assume that means you've got another one?"

He nodded. "That modified pulse radar. I haven't gotten to try it, yet, but she said it was for close-in work. This seems to fit that description. We can use that to get a better sense of the station from out here."

"Will that work?" I asked Mikey.

She nodded. "Yes. It's pretty much what it was designed for. But—"

She paused.

"Yes?" I prompted.

"But it's kind of like ringing their door bell," she said. "After all, their scanners will pick up our pulse. They'll know we're out here, and that we know they're there."

"If there's anyone there," I said. "Place looks pretty dark to me."

"Besides," Jamie said, "they know already. We picked them up on hyperwave. They'd see us the same way."

"No," Mikey shook her head. "At least, probably not. We're a tiny gravity source, and Tom's got us moving slowly. We're not kicking up large enough waves to be noticed. And as for your point," she turned to me, "it's a good one. There probably isn't anybody on board that station. But that's your call. You're the captain. I'm just pointing out the risks."

Her words hit me like a blow. I had never

honestly thought about it like that. I mean, in all the trips Jamie and I had taken, flitting about the system for six hours at a time, all our decisions had been joint ones. I'd never thought of the responsibilities of captaincy applying to a little runabout like this one.

Obviously, though, as she'd pointed out, I was wrong.

I nodded, thinking over what they'd both said. While I thought, I matched orbits with the station, making sure we stayed well back from it. If we were going to be cautious, I decided, we better not get any closer.

There wasn't all that much to think about. I felt we were all pretty much in agreement that the station was merely an old derelict. Still, this was my first real "command decision," and I wanted to do it right.

"Prepare for pulse," I said, "on my mark."

Jamie turned to Mikey. While she showed him how to operate it, I turned the ship so its tail pointed at the station. I also set the controls for emergency acceleration. I really didn't think anyone would respond to our knock, but if they did I wanted all my options ready.

Jamie's hands stilled, his finger poised over a button, and I knew he was ready.

I gave him a wink, took a deep breath, and said, "Mark."

His finger stabbed the button and our pulse went out into the deep, dark night of space.

Chapter Sixteen

Nothing happened. I think we all let out a collective sigh of relief as I eased my finger away from the panic button.

"Scan ready, Captain," Jamie said, peering at the images on his screen. Beside him, Mikey leaned over and started pointing things out. I was glad to see the two of them working so well together. Then I had no more time to watch them as I started easing us closer to the station.

"Looks empty, all right," he said a few minutes later. "Our pulse went all the way through it, and there's not a sign of life. Here's the interesting thing, though: according to our scan, the station is fully functional. Its main systems are off line, but not completely shut down. It looks to be in standby mode. Communications are down, as are the nav beacons and the station computers, but the whole thing is solar powered so it could be restarted quickly."

I frowned. "Are you suggesting we start it up?"

He chuckled. "No, sir."

I thought I detected a slight emphasis on the "sir," and found myself chuckling, too.

"I'm pointing out," he continued, "that it's odd for anyone to abandon a station and leave it intact behind them. The salvage on a place like this might not be much, but surely it would be something."

Beside him, Mikey nodded. "And, too, where there's power, there might be air."

"Meaning?" I asked.

"Meaning that we might not need our suits to explore the station," she said.

"And no one would have to know," Jamie added.

I paled slightly, my good humor vanishing at the thought. "You're talking about docking."

They both nodded, not seeing my point.

I sighed. "In the first place, you said the equipment was operational; you did not say it was up and running, which means there will be no station computer to guide us in. For that matter, there will be no one to run the station side of things: securing hook-ups, opening hatches, bleeding air out of the lock, and so on."

"There'll be manual switches," Jamie said, "ways to dock when the power is out."

I nodded. "In the second place," I went on, as though he'd never spoken, "I've never done a docking before. These runabouts may not be all that big, but docking maneuvers are pretty delicate. I've never even done them on a simulator."

Jamie looked at me, a familiar look on his face. "Scared?" he asked.

I gave him a small smile. "You bet," I said. "Only a fool wouldn't be."

Then I glanced at Mikey. She, too, was looking at me, but the expression on her face was a lot harder to read. "I'm not worried," she said.

I didn't have an answer for that.

I looked at the two of them, Jamie grinning wildly, Mikey staring back with a sort of calm confidence on her face, and I knew I didn't have to put this one up for a vote. They both wanted to try it.

And so did I, I realized.

I sighed, turning back to my controls so they wouldn't see the sudden smile on my face. "Give me a closer look at those docking rings," I said. "I want to know what we're up against before we get there."

Jamie let out a little whoop and bent over his controls. Mikey only smiled softly, nodded, and then turned to help him.

Me, I just grinned a little wider, and concentrated on bringing us ever closer to the abandoned space station.

Chapter Seventeen

The central core of the station was aligned with Antillus' axis, so naturally we named the top "North" and the bottom "South." We were coming in from above, if only slightly, so I selected the northern docking ring to try my skills on. Jamie and Mikey provided me with all the information I asked for. The rest was up to me.

"Two minutes to contact," I announced. "Any advice would be appreciated, but give it soon. Once we close to within ten meters, I won't want the distraction."

Jamie just shook his head. Mikey looked for a moment like she was going to say something, then she changed it to a smile and said, "You can do it, Tom."

I smiled back, wishing for some of her confidence.

We were barely moving. I was approaching as slowly as I could to give myself lots of reaction time and to minimize damage in case I goofed, but to me it looked like that station was fairly leaping out of the screens at me. All too soon the moment was at hand.

I'd lined us up with the docking port on the way in. The docking ring was like a giant donut with spokes radiating in toward the core. Each spoke was a port. I could see the hatch leading into the station, and I had to match ours up with it. There was a little extendable tunnel built into our ship— as there was in all small craft—that we could seal against the station's hull to prevent air loss. The thing was, the tunnel could only extend out about a meter, which didn't give me a lot of room for error.

Fortunately, things went smoothly for once. I eased us in, using just the barest hint of retros to bring us to a stop, and then checked my readings. We were within half a meter of the station's hatch.

Not bad, I thought. Not bad at all.

"Extend airlock," I said.

Jamie and Mikey both looked at each other. I merely waited, letting them work it out.

I couldn't see Jamie's face; he was turned away from me. Over his shoulder, I could see Mikey, face impassive, meeting his gaze. They held this tableau for maybe twenty seconds before I saw Jamie's shoulders slump slightly. "Go ahead," he muttered.

Mikey smiled, then, but she shook her head. "No, Jamie. I'm the navigator. Tom's the captain. I guess that makes you the first officer. It's your job, if you want it."

Even without being able to see his face I could see him brighten at that.

"Hey," he said, "you're right. How about that?"

He raced over toward the hatch and pulled the lever that extended our airlock. I probably should have spent a moment worrying about that—it was the first time we'd ever used the extensor tunnel—but I didn't have time. Mikey had caught my gaze and given me a wink and a smile, and I found I didn't have room in me just then for concern.

"Lock established," Jamie announced. "Should I open the hatch?"

A sudden look of alarm touched Mikey's face, but I was already responding. "Negative. We'll put on our suits, first. Just because there should be air in that station, doesn't mean that there is. Suits on, but don't seal them unless we have to. That way we won't burn any oxygen."

Mikey nodded her approval and I was surprised at how good that little gesture made me feel.

Then I had to turn away, as Jamie handed me a suit.

They were functional things, not decorative. Jamie got them from a locker near the hatch. We'd counted them before, and knew there were six in there, all of them of the one-size-fits-all variety. The helmets looked like large fish bowls and smelled stale, but they were a lot better than breathing vacuum.

It didn't take us long to get into them. Soon enough, we were grouped before the hatch.

"Tell me again," I said to Mikey, "what that modified pulse radar won't pick up."

She looked at me steadily. "It won't pick up atmosphere, sir," she said. "It will register anything solid."

"So we can be sure that there's no one standing on the other side of that hatch?" I asked.

She nodded. "That's right."

"Good," I said, but I still would have felt better with a blaster in my hand.

"Prepare to seal helmets," I said.

Everyone raised their left hands to the neck seals. I took a deep breath, looked around one more time, then nodded to Jamie.

"Do it," I said.

He took a deep breath, reached out, and pulled the lever. The airlock hissed, then slowly started to swing open.

Chapter Eighteen

As things go, this was pretty anticlimactic. The hatch swung open silently. Jamie stuck his head out, then pulled it back in and gave his report.

"It's a tight seal, Captain. No leaks."

I nodded. "Can you see how to open the station hatch?"

He stuck his head out again for a moment. "Yes, sir. At least, I think so. There's a handle here, anyway, right at the edge of their hatch. Should I pull it?"

I looked over at Mikey but she had nothing more to offer than that calm, confident, supportive stare.

"Pull it," I said. "But—"

I was going to tell him to close our hatch, first. That way, if there was no air in the station, we wouldn't lose everything in our shuttle. I never got the chance. Even as I started to say it, I heard the creak of old metal and knew that he had given it a yank.

I braced myself, waiting for the sounds of violent decompression, but nothing happened. All I heard was a faint pop and a gentle hiss that stopped after two or three seconds, and then Jamie stuck his head back in our craft.

"Hatch open, sir. Readouts show the air is breathable. Permission to unsuit?"

I shook my head at that. "Denied. We'll explore, but we'll keep our suits on, in case of an accident. And we'll seal the ship behind us."

Maybe I was still taking this command thing too seriously, but I reasoned, "better safe than sorry," especially as long as it was going to be my fault if anyone was sorry.

"Ready?" I asked. "Let's go."

Chapter Nineteen

It was old. It was abandoned. And it was one of the neatest things I'd ever seen. Even neater, in some ways, than the caverns where we had our hideaway.

I'd given us three hours for exploration. After that, no matter what, we headed back to Brighthome, if for no better reason than simple courtesy. The folks back there knew when we'd left, and knew the flight limitations of our craft. We weren't burning any fuel, of course, and could have stayed there for days, but no one on Brighthome knew that. After six hours, they'd start to worry. They might even send another shuttle after us—there were signalling systems added to all the Brighthome craft for just such an event— and I already knew that we didn't want to share this find with anyone else.

Not until we had to, anyway.

We stayed together as we went through the abandoned relic. It was clear early on that our first guesses as to the layout had been correct. The two donuts were simply docking rings, with small cargo bays spread throughout. It was the connecting cylinder that held the operational areas, and it was these areas that captured our interest.

For one thing, we couldn't figure out what the station had been used for. Two large docking rings meant lots of traffic, but there wasn't enough storage for this to serve as a good dropping-off point. There were several bunk rooms, but again not enough to handle the traffic that the docking rings indicated. Unless the ships weren't carrying cargo, and the crew never left the ships.

But it was the command center, right in the very heart of the cylinder, that held the real surprises. There were detection devices that made our newly-discovered prizes about the runabout seem like toys. Deep space radar, a passive sensor array that could pick up our runabout on the other side of the system, and a hyperwave grid capable of detecting ships more than a parsec away. And those were just the things that I recognized. Then, too, there seemed to be more communications equipment than any mere space station should need.

What we didn't find were weapons. At least, Jamie and I didn't find any, but then we wouldn't have recognized a multiaxis blaster array if it had been labelled. If Mikey knew more than us—or if she found anything she thought might be a weapon—she didn't say so.

As we searched, I found myself growing less and less confident. The thing was, Jamie's earlier assessment was right. Everything was shut down, but everything was in place. What was more, the whole station had been left in standby mode, ready to return to full operational status with the flicking of a few switches.

I didn't like it. All the signs pointed to the fact that the owners could return at any moment, and somehow I didn't think they'd be pleased to find us here. I mean, what had we found: a station left on standby mode, a station that apparently no one in the entire system knew anything about. Who would want such a thing? What good would it be?

To me, there was only one possible answer: pirates.

I kept my observations to myself, however. Knowing Jamie, he'd want to stick around and meet them. Jamie, like most of the kids on Brighthome, seriously wanted to be a freebooter when he got off Brighthome.

I glanced over at Mikey, who was studying a control panel before her, and found myself thinking, *What does she want?*

There were no answers to that, and I went back to my own explorations.

Chapter Twenty

"I wonder how old that station is?"

Mikey asked the question. We were back aboard our ship, preparing to break away. The three hours I'd allotted us had flown by, fortunately without incident, and now we were trying to figure out just exactly what we'd found.

I was busy at the controls, so Jamie answered her. He was standing over by the airlock, ready to retract the tunnel on my signal.

"Tom tell you about the mining settlement?" he asked.

She shook her head.

"Well, there's this ghost town on Brighthome, on the other side of the moon from the Youth Center. The story is that it's an old mining settlement, left over from the days when people thought they could get rich off Antillus. The original planetary survey noted a lot of unusual crystalline compounds in the planet's crust, and a lot of people came here looking for gems. They didn't find any—or at least no more than normal—and soon went off to greener pastures. Anyway, Antillus doesn't have a breathable atmosphere—not if you like oxygen, anyway—so the mining company terraformed Brighthome to use as a base. My guess is that this station dates back to then, too. Maybe this was a temporary home for them while they 'formed the moon.'"

I pursed my lips and nodded silently. It was a good guess, I thought. Maybe even better than my pirate theory, except I would have expected to find more cargo space. Certainly it was more comforting, although it still didn't explain why they would have left all the equipment when they abandoned it. Unless, of course, they thought they might return some day. But why?

"Is the station hatch closed?" I asked. I could see that ours was.

"Aye, sir," he said.

"Disconnect."

He pulled the lever and we listened to the whir of the extensor tunnel retracting. A moment later there was a faint thud and the whirring stopped.

"Disconnected," he said.

I nodded and started backing away from the station. I could have lifted straight up, but I didn't want my flames to wash across the hull beneath us. Better to play it slow and safe, I thought. Always.

Jamie stowed the suits while I opened up some distance, getting ready to turn us on our tail and light out for home. Mikey, in the meantime, was working the scanner controls.

Suddenly she said, "There's a ship coming in, Captain, out of hyperspace."

"What?" I demanded. "Where?"

"It's still pretty far out, but it's heading straight in."

At that moment her scanner board lit up like a Christmas tree. I thought I heard her swear under her breath, but all she said aloud was, "We just got pulsed."

Jamie and I looked at each other.

"Pirates," I said.

"The miners," he said. "Get us out of here."

That sounded like good advice. I stood us on our tail and hit the jets, heading for Brighthome.

Chapter Twenty-One

"Bad idea, Captain," Mikey said seconds after I hit the panic button. "I'm sorry."

"What do you mean?"

She gestured toward the screen. "I misspoke. We weren't pulsed. That is, we caught the fringe of a standard, system-wide scan. It wasn't aimed at us. In fact, we're small enough, and that probe originated far enough away, that we probably would have gone undetected."

I looked at her. "You say we 'would have' gone undetected. Does that mean—"

She nodded. "As soon as you hit those jets. F equals M A, Captain, even in hyperspace. That acceleration made our ripples big enough that I'm sure we've been spotted."

Neither of us looked at Jamie. Not that it was his fault. He only made the suggestion. I was the one who acted.

"So they've spotted us," I said.

She nodded.

"What about the station?" I asked.

She shrugged. "If they didn't know about it already, whoever they are, then they probably still don't. It's pretty small, it's not moving very fast, and it's in a low orbit around a much larger gravity well. I doubt they'll notice it, unless they get curious about us and backtrack our flight path."

"Should I evade?"

"No. Sir. That would only make them suspicious. They'd almost certainly come sniffing our back trail, then."

I nodded. It made sense. "So what do you suggest?"

"To be honest, sir, I don't think we've got much to worry about. After all, we didn't really do anything wrong. Just explored an old, abandoned space station. We may have broken a few Brighthome rules, but we didn't break any laws."

"Jamie?"

He turned to look at me, a sullen look on his face. "I don't want to give you any more bad advice, Captain, sir."

I glared at him. "Come on, knock that stuff off. I'm at least as much to blame as you are, buddy. *I'm* the one who hit the jets, not you. Let's just say we both got a little nervous, okay? Now come on. I need you on this."

He frowned, but I could see he was starting to think again. After a moment he nodded. "She's right, Tom. I don't think there's much to worry about. Unless, of course, that's a pirate ship, in which case there's not much we can do."

Now it was Mikey's turn to frown. "Pirates? Really?"

I nodded. "It could be. Rumors, you know? We hear about them around here sometimes, though how much of it is true and how much just wishful thinking is hard to tell."

"Don't you think we should call for help?" she said. "I hate to suggest it, but—"

"Forget it," Jamie said. "If it is pirates, they'll jam our signal as soon as we open it, and all we'd accomplish is letting them know we're on to them. No, I vote for your first suggestion: let's just head home, though I'd keep us on maximum burn all the way."

When did this turn back into a democracy? I wondered. Still, considering the import of what was happening, I was just as glad to share the responsibility again.

"Can anyone give me a position report on that ship?"

Mikey and Jamie both bent to the scanner controls, working together again. After a moment, Jamie announced, "It's still in hyperspace and coming in fast, but it's altered its course slightly. It's coming right at us."

"How soon?"

He glanced at Mikey who pointed to something on his board. "Intercept in eight minutes," he said.

I glanced at my own board. We wouldn't reach Brighthome for another fifteen minutes. "They've got us," I said. "If they want us, there's nothing we can do."

The words had barely left my mouth when one of the consoles lit up again, but this time it wasn't a radar pulse. It was something almost as rare on a Brighthome shuttle: a communicator signal.

"Looks like they want us," Mikey said.

Beside me, I heard Jamie say, "Maybe it *is* pirates." His voice was too soft for me to be sure, but I could have sworn he sounded hopeful.

Chapter Twenty-Two

"Open a channel, Navigator," I said.

For the first time, I saw Mikey hesitate. "Me? But shouldn't Jamie—"

"It's your board," I said, surprised that I had to explain it to her. "Now open a channel, Navigator, and find out what they want."

She sighed, but pressed the proper buttons. "Brighthome Youth Center shuttle, *Hobo One*. Who is signalling?"

There was a pause, and then we heard a man's voice come over the speaker. "Alex? But I thought—"

"This is Michaela Delacourte, of Brighthome Youth Center," she cut across his voice. "I repeat, who's signalling?"

Another pause, then the same man said, "My apologies, *Hobo One*. This is the Space Guard cruiser *Daedalus*, on routine patrol in this sector. What's your hurry?"

"How's that, *Daedalus*?"

"I said, what's your hurry, *Hobo One*? One moment you weren't there, the next moment you hit our hyperwave detectors like a boulder in a small pond."

"No problem, *Daedalus*. It's just that we're kind of late getting back. Didn't want mama to worry."

She put a wry note in her voice as she said that last part and we heard him chuckle in response. "That's a roger, *Hobo One*. Haven't seen any pirates in the neighborhood, have you?"

"Negative, *Daedalus*. Is that why you're here? Pirate hunting?"

The humor was gone from his voice as he answered, "We've heard rumors of increased activity in the area. We just want to maintain a presence, so let us know if you see anything, all right?"

"Affirmative, *Daedalus*. Good hunting."

"Thanks, *Hobo One*. Do you need an escort?"

"Negative. ETA in—" She glanced at me.

I held up a hand showing five fingers.

"—five minutes," she said. "I think we can make it."

"Roger, *Hobo One*. *Daedalus* out."

The speaker clicked off. Mikey settled back in her chair and let out a sigh.

"The Space Guard?" Jamie said. "Here? I wonder why."

But all I could think about was that name. Alex? What did it mean?

Chapter Twenty-Three

It was Mikey who brought us back to business.

"Hey, guys," she said, "I know that was pretty exciting and all, but don't you think we should get busy? We'll be on the ground in a few minutes. Don't we need to get the security lockouts back in place and all?"

Jamie and I looked at each other and then he leaped for the panel at the back of the cabin. She was right. He had to reset the computer, and he didn't have five minutes to do it in, either. He had less than two, unless I wanted to hit the atmosphere with the ship on manual, with no computer back up.

I gripped my controls and watched my screens, waiting for them to come back on line.

"Is flying with you always this much fun?" Mikey asked, and I was surprised to hear real humor in her voice. Either she didn't know how risky this was, or she was a lot braver than I was.

Or else she was a very good actress.

"Navigator," I said, eyeing the fuel indicator. "Plot us a course. Any course. Just make sure that the round trip will consume that much fuel," and I pointed to the indicator. "Feed it to the computer when Jamie tells you to. He'll lock it in from back there." Her hands were already flying across her controls, and again I marvelled at her skills.

My screens came to life about then, and moments later she lifted her head and nodded toward me. "Good job," I said. "Jamie? Ready to set a new course into the log?"

"Just a moment," he called back, then, "Go."

I didn't wait to see her respond. We were entering the atmosphere, and my flying took all of my concentration. I did hear her close the panel over the scanner controls, though, and I smiled to myself.

Jamie and I had made a good team, but with Mikey we were even better.

I was still grinning when we touched down on Brighthome.

Chapter Twenty-Four

My good humor didn't last long, however. For one thing, Mikey was all excited about everything that had happened. She could hardly wait for the three of us to grab some lunch and then head over to the caves to talk about our day.

And I agreed with her; under other circumstances, I would have been eager to do that myself. But these weren't other circumstances.

"That was incredible," she was saying as we popped open the hatch and stepped out into the hangar.

I didn't know whether she was talking about exploring the station or talking with the Space Guard. Either way, she was right.

"Hey, Frank," Jamie said, greeting the maintenance man as he came over toward us. He made a habit of checking each craft over as soon as it came in.

Frank nodded to us, but didn't say a word as he squeezed past us into the open hatch. Mikey was the only one who was surprised. Glancing back, I saw that he was already closing the airlock behind him.

"Frank's a good guy," I said, placing my hand on her arm to draw her attention to me, "but he doesn't talk much, and not at all to strangers. I don't know why, but he seems to get along with machines a lot better than with people."

I didn't know his story. Learning it was one of the things I hoped to do before I left Brighthome. He seemed to be in his forties, and in the last few weeks he'd finally gotten to where he trusted Jamie and me enough to say hello to us when we met in the hangar. I was pretty sure it was Mikey's presence that had sent him back into his shell.

"So," Mikey said as we headed out into the sunshine, "what's the plan?"

This was the part I hadn't been looking forward to. Jamie looked over at me, his eyes once again hooded and distrustful.

"I'll tell you what," I said to her, "Jamie and I have some things to do. Why don't we all meet for supper? We can head over to the campsite afterwards and talk. What do you think?"

She had stiffened at my words. Now she stopped, just outside the doorway, and turned to look at me. I couldn't read the expression on her face, but I thought I saw disappointment there, disappointment and maybe even a little pain. I wanted to reach out to her, wanted to take back my words, but I couldn't. I had promised Jamie we'd spend this time together, alone, and I couldn't hurt him again.

All she said, though, was, "Fine. I'll see you then."

Glancing over toward Jamie, she gave him a little salute, then turned and walked off.

I felt as though she'd taken a little piece of me with her, but I forced a smile as I, too, turned toward Jamie. "Well, buddy," I said. "What should we do? Got any new vid games we could try?"

The grin fell off my face just then, however. I'd been watching Mikey out of the corner of my eye. As she neared the corner of the hangar, a figure stepped out from around the corner and blocked her path. I recognized the figure immediately: it was Burles, and he didn't look happy.

Chapter Twenty-Five

I thought Mikey was going to attack him. I certainly would have, if I'd been her, rather than waiting for him to make the first move. Burles was too big, too mean, to give any advantages to him. She didn't, though. She just came to a halt, barely out of his reach, and put her hands on her hips. I did notice, however, from the way she had her legs braced, that she was ready to leap into action at the first sign of a threat.

For a moment nothing happened, which gave Jamie and me time to catch up to Mikey. I had no idea what we would do if he tried anything, but I sure wasn't just going to stand back and watch.

Surprisingly, Burles' first words weren't directed at Mikey, or even at me. The first thing he said was, "You with them, Jamie?"

Beside me, I felt Jamie hesitate. What was going

on? I wondered. He spoke up, though, before I could even think of who to ask that question of.

"Yeah, I guess I am," he said. "Tom's my best friend, Burles. You know that."

"And the girl?" There was no emotion in his voice, nothing to clue me in to what he was thinking, or what they were talking about.

"Yeah, she's all right."

Burles looked at him for a moment longer. "You know this hurts your chances, don't you?"

Jamie sighed. "Yeah, I guess. On the other hand, though, what good would I be if I didn't stick up for my friends?"

That seemed to catch Burles off guard. He started to say something, stopped, then started again, which was when Mikey spoke up.

"Hey," she said, "if this is a private conversation, we'll be glad to leave you two alone. On the other hand, if you've got business with me, let's get to it."

He turned his attention to her, and I found I did not like what I saw in his eyes. "Yeah, lady," he said, "I got business with you, but now's not the time to take care of it. Nah, I just wanted to make sure you had a good trip. No surprises or anything. You know, those shuttles are pretty old. Almost anything could go wrong with any of them. Spacers like yourselves could get stranded out there, with no way to get home."

He held her gaze, and it was like watching two giants playing at tug-of-war. Neither of them so much as moved, but there was this air of tension stretching between them.

It was Mikey·who broke the silence. "Yes, well, thank you for your concern, but as you can see we

made it back safe and sound. And we'll make it back
next time, too, no matter what might happen."

A smile twisted his mouth, and it was not a nice
smile. "I hope so, lady. Like I said, we got business."

He held her gaze for another five, maybe ten seconds, then suddenly spun on his heel, and walked
away.

As soon as he rounded the corner, Mikey sagged
back on her heels, her shoulders slumping as the
tension went out of her.

"Wow," I said. "Did he just do what I think he
did?"

"You mean threaten to do something to our
shuttle? Yeah," Mikey said, "I think he did."

I turned to ask Jamie what he thought, and to
grill him about what he and Burles had been talking
about, but as soon as I met his eyes he gave me a
little head shake. I frowned, but kept quiet, though
I tried to send him a signal with my eyes: "We'll
talk later," I told him silently.

He nodded. He didn't look happy about it, but
he nodded.

"Come on," I said. "Let's all go get some lunch."
Considering what had just happened, I didn't think
Jamie would say a word about Mikey joining us.

I was right.

Chapter Twenty-Six

"So, you want to tell me what that was all about?"

Jamie and I were alone at our campsite. Mikey had eaten lunch with us, but the tension between my best friend and me must have been pretty obvious. She'd been quick to turn me down when I'd asked her to come along to the caves.

Of course, she'd also been pretty quick to refuse when I'd offered to walk her back to her dorm. "Thanks, Tom," she'd said, "but I can't let Burles intimidate me. If I start feeling like I need a bodyguard, then he's already defeated me. You can see that, can't you?" and she'd laid her palm briefly against my cheek.

I'd wanted to tell her that I wasn't trying to be her bodyguard—heck, after seeing how she handled Burles the other day, I figured she was better at that stuff than I was. I just wanted to spend a little more time with her.

I couldn't say that, though, so she walked off alone and I ended up at our campsite, trying not to take my frustrations out on Jamie.

He was leaning up against one of the walls. He had one of his handheld vid games in his lap and was playing with it. I didn't think he'd turned it on yet, but he was running his fingers over the controls, tracing the screen, things like that.

Jamie looked up when I spoke, flinching either from my words or my sharp tone. Sitting against the stalagmite in the center of the room, I watched him decide how to answer me. Would he play it straight, I wondered, or would he try something like, "What was what all about?"

As it turned out, he found a third option. After meeting my gaze for something like ten seconds, he sighed and dropped his eyes back to the game in his lap. "I can't tell you," he said in a very small voice.

"What? Jamie—" That stung. First, I strike out with Mikey, and now my best friend for the past two years is keeping secrets from me. I felt like there was this giant bubble building inside of me, a pressure that started in my belly and was pressing up into my chest, and I didn't know how to get rid of that feeling.

"They made me promise," he said, still looking down.

I couldn't help myself. The words came out before I even realized what I was saying. "So your promise to someone else is more important than me?"

His head jerked up and I could see the blood drain from his face. "No, I—"

Immediately I felt bad about what I'd said, but

I couldn't take the words back. I couldn't even apologize for them. It was just like being unable to tell Mikey how I felt: some things you just can't do. Instead, I tried to find a way around it.

"All right," I said, making a sort of waving off gesture with my right hand, "what can you tell me? I mean, come on, Jamie, you know what Burles did to Mikey, and you know what he wants to do to her. Now I see you carrying on a real palsy conversation with him. You have to tell me something."

His face was still pale and his voice was still small, but this time he didn't drop his gaze when he nodded and said, "All right. Actually, I'd be surprised if you didn't know about them already, what with you being pirate kin and all."

And that's when it hit me. That's when suddenly everything made sense. "Wait a minute," I said, thinking furiously, remembering back to a day a year earlier when some clowns had approached me. "Did these guys say they were pirates? No, wait. Not pirates. Did they say they were *going* to be pirates, someday?"

He could see what I was doing. All he had to do was nod or shake his head. That way, he wasn't really breaking his promise to them. That was one thing about Jamie—for all the trouble he'd gotten into in the past, and it had to have been a lot for him to end up here, he absolutely would not tell a lie. That was why my words to him earlier had been so unfair.

He nodded, but I could tell by how slow he did it that I didn't have it all yet.

"All right," I said, "and then they said you could be a pirate, too, if you joined up with them, right?"

He nodded again, quicker this time.

"And you believed them?" There was no scorn in my voice. Only sadness.

He looked away this time before nodding a third time.

I could see it, for Jamie and for so many of the other kids here. Brighthome really was a last chance for a lot of people. For some, though, by the time they got here, it was already too late.

Jamie was one of those. Not that he was a bad kid. He wouldn't have been my best friend if he was, but there was a lot of stuff in his past that would work against him later. I don't mean the pranks he pulled that got him sent here. All that kind of stuff was sealed up when people left here, supposedly anyway, and not opened up again unless they got into trouble. The thing was, I knew Jamie's dreams. They weren't too far off from mine. He wanted space, wanted to sail the stars in a perpetual night, to set his feet on new worlds, and maybe— that most elusive dream of all—maybe be on the ship that first found another intelligent species out there.

He wanted all that, just as badly as I did, but his chances of having any of it weren't good. Space was hard to get into, at least on any decent terms. Oh, little ships like the shuttle we flew were commonplace, but you couldn't use a runabout to explore the galaxy. They simply didn't have the range. There were ships that were built for that, but there weren't many of them, and none of them had kids like us on them. The merchants, those ships that sailed from colony to colony and sometimes made little exploratory side trips, were pretty clannish. They tended to be family-run businesses, and the only way outsiders could get in was to buy in: invest in the business, become a partner, and then you could ship out with them. People like Jamie and me would never have that kind of money.

Which left, really, only two options: the Space Guard and the pirates. The Space Guard had rules, a rigid lifestyle, and all the other things most of the kids here had already rebelled against. The pirates—or so everybody believed—just had fun.

It was no wonder so many kids dreamed of being a pirate one day. Sailing the sea of stars sure beat the heck out of drudge work five days a week, and any dream was better than no dream at all.

So, sure, I could understand it, and I hadn't laughed at those kids when they'd come to me a year ago. They had their dream; it was just that it wasn't my dream. And I didn't laugh at Jamie, either. I merely told him the same thing I said to them.

"Jamie," and now it was my voice that was soft and low, "my friend, let me ask you something. Do you think that real pirates, that Old Jack himself, would bother with us? This is Brighthome, Jamie, a glorified juvenile detention center, and while we may kid ourselves, calling it 'the Penal Colony to the Stars,' that's still all it is: a glorified juvenile detention center."

"Yeah? So?" His color had come back, and his voice had strengthened. Here I thought I was letting him down gently and all I'd done was make him mad. "Don't you see, Tom, that that makes this exactly the kind of place that the pirates *would* look for recruits? Heck, half their work has already been done for them. Most of the kids here already *want* to be pirates, and we've all proven ourselves. I mean, we've all broken the law in some way. I think we'd make perfect pirates, and I think Old Jack himself would agree." He didn't seem mad anymore, if indeed he ever had been. Maybe what I'd thought was anger was simply intensity, a seriousness I'd rarely seen in him before.

I sighed. He had a point. But I still didn't believe it.

"Besides," he went on, "there are all those stories."

I'd been waiting for that. It was darn near impossible to talk about pirates without somebody mentioning those stories. Rumor had it that every once in a while a runabout from Brighthome would disappear. It hadn't happened in all the time I'd been there, and I'd never spoken with anyone who had firsthand knowledge of a disappearance, but still the stories persisted.

"All right," I said, unwilling to argue about those. After all, even though I didn't believe the stories were true, I couldn't disprove them. "But we're getting off the subject here. I'm not claiming the pirates don't exist, or even that they don't operate in this sector sometimes. Heck, we saw that just today, with our run-in with the Space Guard. That cruiser wouldn't be here if the pirates weren't real. What I am saying, Jamie, is that I don't think any of the kids here on Brighthome are pirates, no matter what they may say."

He held up his hand. "Wait a minute, Tom. They didn't say they were pirates."

I blinked at that. "What?"

He shook his head. "They said they're *going to be* pirates. They plan to commandeer a shuttle at some point and go out looking for them, and they offered to take me along."

I blinked again. "They what? They're going to take

a broken down old shuttle and try and find the pirates? They're going to try something the entire Space Guard has been unable to do?"

"No," he shook his head again, his face completely serious. "The Space Guard is trying to find the pirates' base. All these guys want to do is make contact with a single pirate ship. It shouldn't be that hard. Just get away from Brighthome and send out a signal."

I sighed. "Jamie, I think we just figured out what happened to the ships in all those stories. They didn't get hijacked by pirates. They got lost out among the stars, that's all."

He just looked at me, and I knew we'd come to that point where there were no more words. Logic had brought us this far, each of us pointing out things that we thought might convince the other, but we had just run out of arguments. All we had left were beliefs: he believed one thing, I believed another. One of us was right, one of us was wrong, and we both knew that we weren't going to change the other's mind.

I knew all of that, and I should have dropped it right there, but there was one more question I just had to ask. "So," I said, "Burles is obviously with this group, and you clearly want to be a part of it. What happens when Burles makes his move against Mikey and me? Whose side will you be on?"

He flinched away and I knew I'd hurt him. Before our talk, I would have taken his support for granted. My question made it pretty clear that I didn't feel I could trust him anymore. I couldn't help it, though. For one thing, it was a legitimate question. Besides, he'd kind of hurt me, too, with his talk of joining the pirates. I mean, it was one thing to listen to your friend dream of moving away; it was something quite different to hear him making real plans for it.

He didn't drop his gaze, though, and I felt that bubble within me turn to a block of solid ice as he said, "I don't know, Tom. I honestly don't know."

What could I say to that? I nodded once, rose to my feet, and went out, leaving him with his plans and his dreams and his pain.

Chapter Twenty-Seven

Eventually I ended up back at the library. I wasn't really interested in doing any more research at the moment—after that talk with Jamie, I was in no mood to pursue any dreams of my own—but I couldn't think of anywhere else to go. The cave was my spot to sit and think, which was what I wanted to do the most, but I needed some space from Jamie right now.

I read for a while, taking some comfort in the weight of a book in my hands, and then headed over to one of the smaller workstations. I still didn't feel like looking into any more disappearances, but I thought I'd see what I could find about the history of Brighthome.

Surprisingly, I didn't find anything, or at least nothing I didn't already know. This place had been a mining base, had been shut down, and then reopened as a youth center as part of an expansion of Youth Services in this sector. End of story.

Frustrating. I couldn't help feeling that there should have been more. It would have been neat to find out that the mining company on Antillus had been owned by Old Jack himself, or, even better, had been a front for Space Guard activity in the area, but neither of those were the case.

I grinned. Sometimes even I thought I day-dreamed too much.

Glancing at the display in front of me, I saw that it was time for dinner. Shutting everything down, I returned my book to the stacks and then headed over to the cafeteria.

Inside, I looked first for Mikey and then for Jamie. I didn't see either one of them. Instead, I saw Fritz Laramie sitting at that same table near the back door, but this time he wasn't alone. Two of Burles' cronies were with him, though at least Burles himself wasn't in sight.

I sighed, grabbed a plate of food for myself, and headed over to join him.

"Hey, Fritz," I said, seating myself across from him. "Hi, Loren; hi, Martin," I added to the pi-rate wannabes who sat on either side of Fritz. They were both younger and smaller than he was, but we all knew that, with the threat of Burles behind them, their size didn't matter.

Fritz threw me a grateful look as I sat down, but he didn't say anything. It was Loren, on Fritz's right, who spoke first.

"You shouldn't be here, Jenkins," he said.

I grinned. "Where, Loren? Here on Brighthome, or here at this table?"

He didn't answer me, but Martin said, "Burles

has business with Fritz, you know? And I don't think you want to interfere with Burles' business any more than you already have. So why don't you just take your food and go eat at another table?"

I dropped my grin then and looked at Fritz. "No," I said, "I think I want to eat my dinner right here." It wasn't that I was feeling particularly brave; it was just that I'd realized I couldn't get in any deeper than I already was, and I didn't want to see anyone else get sucked in, too.

"Fine," Martin said. "Fritz was finished anyway, weren't you, Laramie?"

He rose, pulling Fritz to his feet. Loren picked up Fritz's half-empty plate, watching me carefully as though I might try to take it from him.

"Fritz—" I said.

"It's all right," he said, and he sounded calm. If he was afraid, he was covering it up well.

"You don't have to go with them," I said. "We told you—"

"I know," he said, "and I appreciate it, but I really don't have any choice."

There wasn't much I could say to that. I thought he was wrong, but I didn't know how to convince him of that. Fritz nodded once, then allowed Loren and Martin to lead him away.

I frowned, wondering how I could have played that differently, and wishing that Mikey had been there. Was there anything I could have said or done that might have helped?

I couldn't answer those questions. My appetite gone, I picked at my food for a little while, then headed back to my dorm. The whole day was shot, anyway, I thought. I might as well turn in early and hope that tomorrow went better.

Chapter Twenty-Eight

The next day didn't start out any better. It dawned clear and bright, but I woke up to find that Jamie hadn't come in at all. In a way, that didn't surprise me. He hadn't shown up by lights-out, and I'd covered for him when the Prefects came around. We had both done that before, spending nights in the caves—which was one reason why we called that one room our campsite—sneaking out after the Precepts had made their rounds, but this was the first time he'd stayed there without me. So, in a way, it didn't surprise me, but it hurt, more than I would have expected.

On top of that, I couldn't find Mikey anywhere. Not that there were all that many places to look. Actually, there was only one. I mean, I didn't want to go to the caves. I figured Jamie was there, and I didn't want to bump into him like that.

And I couldn't very well go to her dorm looking

for her. That would get people talking, even more
than they already were, and while I wouldn't mind
taking all the kidding if we were actually going
together—

I shook my head and decided to be honest, since
there wasn't anyone else around. The truth was, I
wouldn't mind taking the kidding even if we weren't
going together. Oh, I'd probably make a big show
of being embarrassed and all, but I didn't think it
would really bother me. The thing was, I didn't
know how Mikey would react, especially since we
weren't anything more than friends, and so I
couldn't go to her dorm.

Which left the cafeteria.

For all my good intentions, I hadn't slept very
well the night before, and so I ended up not getting up until about ten, but still I figured I'd find
her there. Sunday brunch was a pretty popular
meal, but when I got to the cafeteria, all show-
ered and in a fresh jump suit, I found the place
practically empty. Just a few kids in there, all of
them loners like me, sitting alone at widely scattered tables.

I grabbed a couple of apples for my own break-
fast, shoved them into my pockets, and headed back
outside.

It should have been a dark, dreary, rainy morning, just to go along with my mood. This was
Brighthome, however, and though the miners—or
whoever—had terraformed it, they hadn't worked
any miracles. It was still a moon, with a diameter
of something like a thousand kilometers, and while
it had gravity and an atmosphere, it didn't have
anything like clouds or rain or weather of any kind.
Just a rocky, grey landscape and perpetual sunshine

during the day, and a whole galaxy full of stars at night.

In the end, I headed over to the hangar. No Mikey, no Jamie, and I didn't feel much like dreaming about the Space Guard, so I decided to try and get some work done. I was still thinking about Burles' thinly veiled threat from yesterday. With nothing else going on, I thought I'd go and inspect the ship, just in case.

The hangar was a low, squat, brick building. I didn't know why most of the Youth Center buildings were brick. Some kind of architectural statement, I supposed. Only one story tall, it was nonetheless a very large structure, running something like a hundred meters square.

The west wall opened onto the landing pad, and had these enormous overhead doors. The south wall, which was the one that faced the Youth Center, only had three smaller doors, one in the middle and one at each end.

I always used the one in the middle. They all had electronic locks, each with a numeric keypad and a thumb-sized scanner, and though I was pretty sure they all used the same access code, I never felt like walking all that way just to find out.

I keyed in my code and placed my thumb on the scanning window and waited for the door to pop open. I could still remember when I'd first received my own personal code, and the first time that door opened for me. It was one of my brightest memories of Brighthome, the day I earned my flames, and I still smiled every time the hangar let me in.

This time, however, my smile didn't stay on my face very long. I took two steps into the building, my eyes automatically searching out my ship, and then I froze. The *Hobo One* was there, all right, but its access panel was open, and someone was bending over with his head and arms in the engine compartment.

Under other circumstances, that wouldn't have been all that surprising a scene. Frank was always working on one or another of the ships. Tinkering, repairing, maintaining, whatever. Those shuttles were his life, and his friends.

These weren't other circumstances, however, because the guy with his hands in my ship wasn't Frank. It was Burles.

Chapter Twenty-Nine

The ship was about twenty paces in front of me. I covered half that distance without having any idea what I was going to do once I got there. I only knew that Burles had his hands where they didn't belong, and I had to do something.

Before I got there, something happened that changed everything. From somewhere deeper in the hangar, I heard Frank's voice call out, "Burles! You got that beastie recalibrated yet?"

That question just stopped me in my tracks. Burles pulled his head out of the compartment and called back, "Just about, Frank! I should have it finished in another minute."

"Well, hurry up about it. We've got three more craft to overhaul before this day is through."

Burles started to bend down again, but then he stopped, set down the tool in his hand, wiped his hands on a dirty rag, and started massaging his lower back. As he did so, he looked around the hangar. It only took a moment or so before he caught sight of me, my mouth hanging open, my hands clenched into fists at my sides.

He grinned. That's all. Just grinned. Then he picked up his wrench and went back to work on my engines.

I spun away, looking for Frank. There were still some things I wanted to say to Burles, but I figured I better check some other things out, first.

Frank was working on another shuttle. He, too, had the engine compartment open, but his movements were a lot quicker and surer than Burles'.

"Frank," I said, keeping my voice low so as not to startle him. He was pretty engrossed in his work and hadn't heard me approach.

Frank was the only staff person on Brighthome that we didn't call "Mister." In fact, I'd never even learned his last name. Now, thinking about who was working on my ship, I found myself hoping his last name wasn't Burles.

He lifted his head out and looked over at me, grunted a greeting, and kept on working.

For Frank, that was about as talkative as he ever got with me. It wasn't that he was mean, or anything; quite the contrary, in fact. He was a likeable old guy, as long as you took him on his own terms. It was just that he wasn't all that comfortable around people. Considering who most of the people were here on Brighthome, I couldn't say that I really blamed him, either.

I had to be careful how I handled this. I'd gotten to where I could talk to him fairly easily about hardware—the fuel consumption rate of my shuttle, why I kept getting a warning light when

I brought her in for a landing, things like that, but the few times I'd tried to talk to him about the other kids, he'd simply withdrawn from the conversation.

"Hey, Frank," I said, a kidding note in my voice, "I see you've got someone else doing your work."

Frank's hands never slowed, and he didn't turn to look at me, but he grunted again.

"He's working on my shuttle. I hope he knows what he's doing." I still had that bantering note in my voice, and Frank surprised me by actually chuckling.

"Nah," he said, "I always let greenhorns recalibrate fuel condensers. If the shuttle blows, that's one less for me to worry about." He chuckled again, then set the wrench down and turned a serious expression toward me. "Burles is a good kid," he said. "Came in here five, six months ago, wanting to earn his flames. Kind of like you did a while back. Got started learning some of the hardware—just like you had to—and found he liked it better than flying. Stayed on as my assistant." He gave me a quick wink. "Good kid," he said again. "Doesn't talk much." And with that he turned away and went back to work.

I could only stand there, shaking my head. I'd known Frank for over a year now, and that little speech was easily the longest one I'd ever heard him make.

Still shaking my head, I turned away and headed back toward my ship, knowing I wouldn't get any more information out of him. As I went, though, I found myself thinking about Burles in an entirely new light. I mean, up until a couple of days ago, he was simply a bully I tried to avoid. Then, after what he tried to do to Mikey, I found myself hating him with a passion that surprised me. Now, though, after hearing Frank talk about him, I didn't know what to think of him. Frank gave his friendship slowly. If Burles had earned it, there must be more to him than I'd seen.

I still hated him; I still wasn't about to let him hurt Mikey; but beyond that I didn't know what to think.

Burles had closed up the engine compartment before I got back. His tools were all back in the box by his feet, and he was wiping his hands on that same dirty rag.

I had the distinct impression he was waiting for me.

As with Frank, I wasn't sure how I wanted to play this. Bluster wouldn't work. I didn't have the size to intimidate him. All that would probably do was earn me a poke in the nose. On the other hand, I couldn't just walk away, either. There were things I had to say to him, if only for my own peace of mind.

As it turned out, the choice wasn't up to me. Burles spoke before I could.

"Hey, Jenkins," he said. "Nice ship."

I nodded. "Try to keep it that way, huh?"

He grinned like I'd just given him the perfect opening. As it turned out, I had.

"Tell that to that girlfriend of yours."

I frowned at that. "What do you mean?"

He shrugged, but his grin got even wider. "Just that Frank and I don't always have time to service every ship the way we'd like, if you know what I mean. Some of them get better attention than others. All I'm saying is, if she decides to be nice to me, well, I could make sure your ship is one that gets the best care. Otherwise . . ."

And here I'd been thinking charitable thoughts about him.

I shook my head, feeling the anger building within me and fighting against it. That was just what he wanted, I knew. For one thing, attacking him like this, I didn't have a chance. He'd get the pleasure of beating my face in, and no one would say a word to him because I started it. In fact, I'd probably get in trouble, in addition to getting the daylights beat out of me.

No, I couldn't do what he wanted, but I couldn't just let it go, either.

"Leave her alone," I said, trying to put as much menace in my voice as I could. "Just leave Mikey alone."

Burles grinned, which told me my menacing voice was about as effective as I'd figured, then he picked up his tools and turned away. He didn't say anything. He didn't need to. Just walked away.

After a moment, I, too, turned away, and headed toward the door. One thing, though, that I made up my mind about as I walked away: I was going to go over every inch of that ship myself before I took it up again.

I stepped out into the bright Brighthome sunshine, knowing what I had to do. Fight or no fight, Jamie needed to know about this, and maybe in talking it over we could patch things up between us.

I was thinking about Jamie, and about Burles, and almost didn't notice Fritz. He was walking toward the hangar from the direction of his dorm. When he saw me, and before I could call out to him, he turned and headed toward the cafeteria.

I didn't know what to make of that, and I didn't have time right then to try and figure it out, so I put Fritz and his troubles out of my mind and set out for the caves.

Chapter Thirty

Things don't always turn out the way I plan. I got to the caverns, all filled with excitement, and looked about for Jamie. I hadn't figured out yet just what my opening words were going to be, but I wasn't too worried about that. I mean, things might be a little strained between us at the moment, but we were still friends.

There was only one thing wrong: Jamie wasn't there. In fact, looking around at our campsite, I could find no sign that he'd been there at all. Jamie was even worse at picking up after himself than I was, but the campsite looked just as it had when I'd left it yesterday. Even his bedroll was unchanged.

I stood there, stunned, looking around me. All right, I thought. He didn't sleep here last night, and he didn't come home. So where was he?

"Jamie," I whispered. "Oh, Jamie, what have you done?"

I looked around again, but there were no answers to be found.

Chapter Thirty-One

Jamie didn't show up the rest of the day, and by the evening I was starting to get a little concerned. I thought that was what he probably wanted, but I couldn't help myself. This was unlike him, and the worst part of it was that I couldn't figure it out. I mean, where was he? This was Brighthome, after all. It wasn't like he had an entire city out there to hide in.

I pretty much stayed in my room all day, hoping to be there when he came in, although I did make a few more trips to the cave. More than anything else, I wanted to be sure he was all right.

I was sitting at our campsite after dinner, idly playing with one of Jamie's vids. He had left this one out, lying on the floor of the cave over by the Christmas Tree. I'd picked it up and started running my fingers over its various buttons and its little screen, but I hadn't turned it on. Jamie was the one who always played with these things. Me, I found just holding it helped me to think about him, and made me feel a little better.

Mostly, though, I was trying to figure out what to do.

I was sitting there like that, back against one wall, vid game in my lap, when I heard the sound of a footfall in the corridor beyond and saw the faintest flickering of lamplight.

"Jamie?" I called, my heart rising to my throat. The funny thing was, now that I knew he was safe, I didn't know whether to feel relieved or angry.

But it wasn't Jamie. It was Mikey. She came out of the tunnel and into our campsite, a concerned look on her face.

"There you are," she said. "I've been looking for you all day."

"There's a lot of that going on," I said. "You haven't seen Jamie around anywhere, have you?"

She shook her head. "No, why? What's up?"

I shrugged. "I don't know. We had a bit of a falling out last night. Nothing big, at least I didn't think so, but I haven't seen him since."

"Don't you two room together?" she asked.

"Yeah. He didn't come home last night."

She had paused just inside the room to talk to me. Now she crossed the ten feet or so between us and sat down next to me. Reaching out, she placed her hand lightly on my knee.

"Do you think he's all right?" she asked.

That was a good question, I supposed, but I didn't like it. I looked away from her, back down at the vid in my lap, and said, "I hope so, Mikey. I hope so."

She gave my knee a little squeeze and then

pulled her hand away. "Where do you think he could be?"

I frowned and set the vid game down before turning back to her. "That's the part that bugs me. I mean, this is Brighthome. It's not like there are a couple of dozen places he could be. There's the Youth Center, there's this place, and there's the old settlement. Beyond that, there's nothing but rock and dust, no place for him to go and no reason for him to go there."

"All right," she said, her brow furrowing slightly, "let's think about what you said. First of all, there's the Youth Center. Could he have bunked with someone else last night?"

My frown deepened. I wondered if she understood what she was really asking: could Jamie have found a new best friend? Well, yes, I suppose he could have, but not that fast.

"I don't think so," I said, trying to answer with my head and not my heart. "I mean, it's possible, but Jamie, for all his clownish nature, doesn't make friends real fast. I don't know if I should tell you this, but both his parents died when he was just a kid. Not at the same time, but within about four years of each other. His dad was the last to go, and Jamie is still kind of mad at him. I know it doesn't really make sense—heck, even Jamie knows that— but he can't help it. It's almost as if he feels that his father left him, and resents him for it."

She thought about that for a moment, and then asked, "Do you think that might be why he's not real friendly toward me?"

I looked at her. "Why? Because he thinks you might take me away from him?"

She nodded.

I thought about it. "I don't know," I said, "but it's a good question." There was a better one, though, one that I didn't have the nerve to ask: *Will you?*

We held eye contact for a few seconds, but I couldn't read anything in her gaze and, in the end, I was the one who looked away.

"Anyway," I went on, "like I said, it's possible, but I don't think so."

"Okay," she said. "What was your second thought? These caves, right? Well, what about that idea? How big is this network of tunnels?"

I shrugged. "I don't know. Big. Jamie and I have explored some of it. We even started making a map last summer, but we didn't get very far."

"Can we go looking for him?"

I had to admit, I liked the way she thought. My inclination was to sit around worrying and feeling sorry for myself; hers was to figure out what to do about it and then go out and do it. For all the tension I was feeling, I found myself wanting to smile in admiration, and wondering if I could learn to do that.

Still, for all that I liked her attitude, I had to say, "No. At least, not practically. The thing is, there are four tunnels that lead deeper in. If that was all, we wouldn't have much trouble, but each tunnel branches several times fairly early on. Jamie and I have gone through maybe a quarter of them, and that took us weeks. We'd never be able to track him, just the two of us."

She didn't like my answer, obviously. She frowned at me but nodded and said, "I suppose you're right. The thing to do would be to get some help, some of the instructors from the Youth Center. They probably have some sensors they could bring in here to help look."

"Do you think we should do that?"

She thought about it for a moment, which kind of surprised me. I thought it was pretty obvious.

"No," she said. "Not yet. Not until we've ruled everything else out."

I nodded. My thinking exactly. I realized then, however, that I had just done her a disservice. I mean, yes, it was pretty obvious, but then I'd been thinking about these very questions before she got here. She was actually picking up the different points very quickly.

"All right," she went on before I could decide whether I wanted to mention that to her or not. "What does that leave us with?"

"The mining settlement," I said.

She nodded. "Right. Do you want to check it out?"

Now it was my turn to think for a moment. For one thing, the settlement was quite a ways away. It would take about forty-five minutes just to walk there. On top of that, it was quite a bit bigger than the Youth Center. We could spend hours going through the place, and still not be sure we'd looked everywhere. In short, we'd be gone most of the day, and if Jamie came looking for us he wouldn't have any idea where we were.

I liked that idea. "Yeah," I said. "I think I do."

She nodded. "Good. I've been curious about that place since you two first mentioned it on the shuttle yesterday. I'd like to see it. But don't you think you should leave Jamie a note, first, just in case he shows up while we're gone?"

Which kind of soured the whole thing for me. I

mean, I didn't mind being a little petty once in a while, but I didn't want her to know that.

"Yeah," I said, not really meaning it. "Good idea," and I picked up the vid I'd been holding. These things had a "TEXT" feature that Jamie normally used when he saved a game without finishing it. He could leave a little description of where he'd left off, in case he didn't get back to it for a few days. I thought I'd use it to leave him a little note, and then leave the vid on his bedroll where he'd be sure to see it.

Pretty clever, I thought.

"I have to ask," Mikey said as I turned on the vid. Her tone had gotten very serious all of a sudden, forcing me to look up again. "This 'falling out' you and Jamie had. Was it over me?"

I smiled, as softly as I could, and reached out to touch her hand. "No, Mikey," I said. "Actually, I think Jamie has pretty much accepted you, especially after you showed him those scanner controls."

She brightened at that, and I dropped my eyes back to the vid in my hands. A single press of a button flipped it over into "TEXT" mode, and I glanced at the little screen as I tried to think of how to phrase my message.

"Well, that's good," Mikey was saying. "I like Jamie."

But I wasn't listening. My eyes were frozen on that little screen.

"What is it?" she asked, when I didn't respond.

"Look," I said, my voice ragged and harsh, and I passed her the vid.

There was a message on the screen. It was a note from Jamie.

Tom:

I guess this is good-bye, old buddy. I wish I could talk to you face-to-face, but you'd probably try to talk me out of this, and my mind's made up. Besides, now that I'm committed, they won't let me talk to anyone outside of the group.

You were wrong, my friend. These guys *are* real pirates, and pretty soon I'm going to be one, too. It's Saturday night, right now. Tomorrow—I don't know what time—we're taking a shuttle and spacing out of here. We're going to hook up with the rest of the pirates and I'm signing on.

I wish we could see each other before I go, but you know what this chance means to me. I've got to take it, and who knows? Maybe you'll change your mind someday and we'll meet up again as brother freebooters.

Gotta go. They let me come back up here to get my vids—they say they can always use someone who knows computers—but I can't take too long about it.

See you around the stars, old buddy.

Your friend,

Jamie

She looked up after reading it, sympathy and concern showing plainly on her face. I could tell she wanted to say something, but I didn't give her a chance.

"Come on," I said, standing up and grabbing her hand.

"Where?" she asked.

"To the hangar. Maybe there's still time. Maybe they haven't left yet."

I was trying desperately to remember how many

shuttles were there when I'd run into Burles earlier. I didn't remember seeing any empty slots, but then I'd been distracted by his presence.

She nodded and rose to her feet. Together, we squeezed out through the tunnel and left the caves on the run.

Chapter Thirty-Two

Running toward the hangar, I realized that I hadn't yet told Mikey—or anyone else—about Burles working on our ship. This would have been a good time to bring it up, except that I was in a hurry and needed all my breath for running.

I had the feeling that Jamie was already gone, but I couldn't let myself slow down.

Mikey kept up with me. In fact, if anything, she was less winded than I was when we slowed to a stop in front of the nearest door. I didn't know if this one would admit me or not, but I was about to find out.

As it turned out, there was no problem. I placed my thumb on the screen and keyed in my code, just like I did at my usual door, and the door popped open for me.

"Come on," I said, and stepped inside the hangar.

It was dark in there, something I wasn't used to.

One thing about having to check out the ships in advance: Frank always made sure that everything was warmed up and ready before I got there.

"Where's the light switch in this place?" Mikey whispered.

"I don't know," I whispered back. I didn't know why we were keeping our voices so low. It was pretty apparent that no one else was in the hangar. It must have been the darkness that prevented us from speaking up.

I dug my little penlight out of my pocket and flipped it on. The glow from my flash didn't help much more than it had in the caves, but at least it made me feel a little better. Mikey must have felt the same way because she stayed close to me as I turned and headed down the aisle between the parked ships.

There were six shuttles, and three other, larger ships that the Youth Center used for various purposes. It didn't take long to run through the list and realize what had happened.

"Tell me," Mikey said as I stopped in front of an empty bay.

I shook my head. "This doesn't make any sense," I said.

"What?" She was standing beside me, hands on her hips, following the beam of my flash.

"This ship. It doesn't belong to anyone." I stopped then, realizing I wasn't telling this right, and took a deep breath. "Look," I began again. "We've got the Hobo One, right? And though you've only been in it once, so you wouldn't know this, every time we ship out we take the same shuttle. It's more of a tradition than a rule—I mean, I suppose I could take any of these, if I wanted, but I'd have to have it keyed over to me, first. They have a pretty good security system here to make sure unqualified kids don't start up a ship they can't handle. Unlike the doors here, I have to ask to have a ship keyed to me, and it's traditional not to ask. Usually, when you earn your flames, you keep the ship you trained on, and it's yours for the rest of your stay on Brighthome."

She nodded. "All right. I'm with you so far. So who's ship is this?"

"That's what doesn't make sense. It isn't anyone's. There are only three of us who are currently rated: myself, and we passed the *Hobo One* when we first came in; Eric, and that's his ship over there;" I pointed with the flash. "I don't know him very well, but he seems all right."

"And the third?"

"Well, that's kind of odd, too. Her name's Carol, and she trained on the larger ships, the ones the Center uses for supply runs, and things like that. She isn't actually checked out on these shuttles. The Center doesn't normally train kids on anything but the shuttles, but she was a special case—I don't know why. Natural aptitude or something, I guess."

Mikey was silent for a moment, thinking. I was silent, too, but only because I'd run out of things to say.

"So," she said, "we have an unclaimed ship missing, and we're pretty sure Jamie's on it."

"That's the way I see it," I said.

"All right. Let's go after them."

I grinned. I couldn't help it. Even though I was going to have to dash her enthusiasm, I couldn't help but admire it.

"We can't," I said, my momentary good humor fading into seriousness.

"Why not?" There was a note of defiance in her voice. "After all, how far could they have gone? It's not like they've got the entire galaxy to roam about in. They've got the same limited range that the *Hobo One* has. We should be able to figure out where they went and go there too."

"We can't," I said again.

"Why?"

"Burles," I said, his name flat on my tongue. "I found out just today that he's been Frank's assistant mechanic here for several months. I came in earlier and found him working on our ship. And you remember what he said yesterday."

She had no immediate response to that. I didn't blame her. I'd been thinking about it for some time, and I still didn't have a response to that.

"Come on," she said, reaching out and grabbing my hand.

"Where?"

"Hobo One."

"But—"

"You'll see." And that's all she'd say until we were inside and at our positions.

"Mikey—" I started, but whatever else I was going to say died on my lips as I saw what she had in mind.

She rolled back the cover from the scanner controls and turned to me. "I need some power for this, Captain."

I nodded and turned to my own controls. One thing about Frank, he may have poor taste in assistants, but he kept his machines in fine form. The *Hobo One* powered up quickly and smoothly, and

I felt the rush of pleasure that always came when the lights came up around me.

My pleasure didn't last long, however.

Mikey's hands flew over her controls. I could see the images on her screen changing too fast for me to read, but the expression on her face was plain.

"Nothing," she said eventually, looking up and meeting my gaze. "I can't find any sign of them anywhere."

I turned away, unwilling to let her see the pain that was on my face. "Oh, Jamie," I said softly. "What have you done, my friend? What have you done?"

She gave me a moment to recover, then said, "All right. We can't track him. Can anyone else here?"

I turned back to her, a spark of hope leaping within me. It died, though, as soon as I thought about it. "No," I said. "Well, yes. I mean, there are these tales floating around about disappearing ships, and so the Youth Center installed tracking devices in all the shuttles, but I don't think they'll do us much good."

"Why?" She was frowning, and I didn't blame her. I didn't like it, either.

"Two reasons. One: because we'd have to convince somebody that there was a problem before they'd do anything, and I don't think we can do that. Sure, *we're* concerned, but anyone else, anyone who doesn't really know Jamie or Burles or any of the others in that pirate group, would just see a group of kids out on a lark. They wouldn't get worried until the six hours had passed."

She nodded. "Good point. What's the other reason?"

"They're pirates, or think they are, and they've

got Jamie on board. I'm sure they could figure out some way to disable the tracking device, if they wanted to."

She nodded again. "All right. So what you're saying is, it's up to us. What are we going to do, Captain?"

There was that enthusiasm again. It hurt me to have to dash it again.

"Not 'we,'" I said. "'Me.' I'm going after them."

"But—"

"Look, Mikey," I said, cutting her off. "I've already pointed out that the only ship I can take is the one Burles had his hands in. There's a good chance that something will happen to it once I get off Brighthome. It looks like I might be about to lose Jamie; I don't want anything to happen to you, too."

She smiled at that, but only for a moment. "Thanks, Tom. I like you, too. But I'm still going. You need a navigator, and you need someone to run the scanner controls. I'm going."

I shook my head. "No, Mikey. I need someone here more. If anything does happen, someone has to be here to tell Frank and the others."

Her hands were still on her controls. Now she crossed them in front of her and said, "Leave 'em a note. I'm going."

I opened my mouth to say something more, but then I closed it and nodded. "All right. Welcome aboard, Navigator. Your first assignment is to get the hangar door open while I run through the pre-flight check. There's a bank of switches on the wall. Take my flash and get that door open."

She never moved. Just sat there, an amused smile on her face. "Nice try," she said, and then she reached over and pressed a button on my console.

Before us, the hangar door slowly lifted.

I sighed and turned back to my controls. "Beginning pre-flight check," I said, wondering why it was that I suddenly felt so good inside.

Chapter Thirty-Three

"I need a course, Navigator."

The blackness of space rolled across the view port before us.

"I need a destination, Captain," Mikey responded.

I gave her a weak nod and sat back in my captain's chair. I'd brought us up here in a hurry, leaving Brighthome within seconds of finishing the pre-flights. Part of it, I knew, was simply that I didn't want Frank—or anyone else—to come in and ask us any questions. Time, I felt, was slipping away, and I didn't want to lose any more.

More than that, however, I didn't want to spend any more time thinking about Burles and what he might have done to the ship. Honestly, I didn't think he'd actually done anything—not with Frank there to check up on him—or I would never have brought Mikey along. No, I didn't think he'd done anything, but I didn't know for sure, and I'd wanted to leave before I thought of any other reasons not to.

And so I'd left, without even a destination in mind.

"Good point," I said. "Any suggestions?"

She shrugged, and flipped one hand toward the view screen. "Out there, somewhere."

"The depths of space, eh?" I thought about that. It was one of the classic guesses for the pirates' hideout: somewhere between the stars, far enough off the travel lanes that no one would stumble across them, but close enough that they could strike when they wanted to. "I don't think so," I said after a moment.

"Why not?"

My turn to shrug. "In a runabout? They couldn't get far enough away in a shuttle."

Mikey frowned. "They could rendezvous with another ship."

I shook my head. "Not with the Space Guard out there."

"The *Daedalus*? But the pirates don't know—"

"Sure they do," I interrupted her. "Jamie's with them, remember? Can you imagine anyone signing up with the pirates and not telling them about a Space Guard cruiser in the area?"

She shook her head.

"So they know about the Guard," I said. "That means that we can rule out any kind of rendezvous. No way they could pull that off without the Guard spotting it."

Mikey thought about that a moment. "So we're looking for something in-system and fairly close, right?"

"Close?" I asked. "How do you figure that?"

She gave me a gentle smile and gestured toward

the scanners she'd first shown us only yesterday. "You just convinced me that they know about the Guard, right? Well, using that same logic, we can assume that Jamie told them how hyperwaves work—if they didn't know already, that is. We're assuming that they want to avoid detection—a pretty safe assumption, I think—which means a small ship, travelling slowly. Anything else—a large gravity source or a small one travelling fast—will show up easily. Just like we did, and you remember how the Guard responded."

"Yeah." I wasn't likely to forget that. "All right. Good point. In-system and close. But where?"

She shrugged again, looking down at the scanner controls. "To be honest, Captain, I see only three choices: one, Brighthome itself."

"Brighthome?"

She nodded. "Yes. Take a shuttle and leave the Youth Center, then turn right around and come back. Maybe land at that old mining settlement. Who would know? Who would even suspect?"

I thought about that. I couldn't see anything really wrong with the idea—in fact, in a way it was kind of clever—but I didn't buy it. Too many kids went in and out of that settlement, even though they weren't supposed to. If there were pirates around, I was pretty sure I'd have heard at least a rumor.

Maybe not, though. I was, after all, pretty much a loner. Maybe there were rumors, and I just hadn't heard them. "What's your second idea?" I asked.

"Antillus," she said. "It's close; it's big; and it's empty."

I nodded, but this one I had an answer for.

"Scratch that," I said. "Not because you're wrong, but because I hope you are. Like you said, it's big. If that's where the pirates are, we'll never find them. So tell me your third idea."

She smiled. "That's the one I like the best: that space station we found yesterday. Think about it, Tom. It's perfect: close, hidden, and it was on standby. All the questions we had when we were exploring it yesterday? They can all be answered by one word: pirates."

Again, I found myself thinking about what she'd said. She was right, it did make a lot of sense, and that was too bad.

"Tom?" she asked, reading the frustration on my face. "What is it?"

I looked over at her. "We've got a problem."

"What? Something wrong with the ship?" Her eyes darted across my board, but there were no red lights showing. I found it interesting, though, that she seemed to be as concerned about that as I was.

"No," I said. "At least, not in that way."

"Then what—"

"We can't go back to the station."

"Why not? It's not that far—" Her voice trailed off, and I saw the sudden understanding in her eyes. "The computer safeguards," she said, her voice flat and empty.

I nodded. "And I don't know how to override them."

She brought her eyes back up to mine, and I was surprised to see pain in hers.

"I do," she said.

"You do?"

She nodded.

"But—"

"I don't have Jamie's skill with computers," she said, her voice still flat and empty. "I can't simply disable them, like he can. I can remove them entirely, but there's no way I can put them back later. Frank will know what we've been up to. It could cost you your flames."

I nodded. She was right. I could get away with a lot, but tampering with the computers would cost me my flames.

"Do it," I said.

She nodded, and started to rise from her chair. She didn't get very far. Before she could even take a single step, the ship started to move. It came about to a new heading, the engines fired, lifted, and we pulled out of our parking orbit.

She reached out for her chair, grabbing on to it for support, and then turned back to me. Whatever she was going to say, however, died, when she saw the look on my face. That, and the fact that my hands weren't on the controls.

"I don't know, Mikey," I said, answering her unspoken question. "I'm not flying this ship, and I don't know who is."

Chapter Thirty-Four

It didn't take us long to find it, once we knew what we were looking for. "There," Mikey said, pointing at a circuit diagram she'd called up on one of her screens. "There isn't supposed to be a break there. Someone's feeding instructions to the computer through that spot."

"Someone?" I snorted. "You mean Burles."

She nodded. "It's the only answer that makes any sense."

I sighed. "All right. Where's the break? And can we plug it?"

She glanced at her diagram again, then called up another schematic. "It's outside," she said. "Access panel N-3."

"That's the main engine access."

She nodded. "The lines run through there. He must have cut into them when he was recalibrating, earlier."

"Yeah. All right, what about my other question? Can we plug it?"

She nodded a third time. "Shouldn't be any problem. He probably left a little radio feeder there, or else a small computer, something that could interface with our own system and feed it signals. It shouldn't be hard to spot it and remove it, but I would prefer having the engines off while I work under there."

"You? But I thought I—"

"No, Captain," she cut me off. "Rank has its privileges, but it also has its responsibilities. Your job is at the controls. Besides, you ever EVA in a moving ship before?"

"No. Have you?" I countered.

"Yes."

I looked at her, and realized that I believed her. I also realized a couple of other things. "Is that something all the senators' children learn on Markus Colony? Or were you a special case, Alex?"

I called her by that name intentionally, and it didn't seem to surprise her. It didn't seem to bother her, either. She merely held my gaze for a moment, then said, "We don't have much time, Captain. Burles didn't plant that device just to inconvenience us. He's got something in mind, and I don't think we're going to like it, whatever it is."

I nodded, once, and dropped my gaze. "Get into your suit," I said.

While she did that, I computed a destination based on our current speed and heading. The results didn't surprise me.

"Well?" she asked, when I sat back in my chair.

"The station," I said. "We're heading straight there."

"ETA?"

"We're doing a slow burn, nothing that will call attention to us. I estimate we'll arrive in fifteen minutes. To be safe, you'd better have that gizmo gone in ten."

She nodded and finished sealing up her suit. A moment later, she was out the lock and gone.

I sighed, and headed over to the suit locker myself. As a precaution—just because I didn't trust Burles at all and didn't know what he had in mind for us—I got into my own suit, but I didn't seal it up just yet. Returning to my chair, I turned back to my useless controls and let out another sigh. Burles had really done a number on us, I had to admit. I had no control over my ship at all. I couldn't even turn off the engines while Mikey worked around them.

Thinking about that, I realized I wasn't particularly worried. I trusted her, and that was kind of a new feeling for me. I knew I would never have let Jamie go out there to work while the ship was moving, rank or no rank. I also knew, however, that when this was all over with, Mikey and I were going to sit down and have a long talk. There were too many things about her, things that I could no longer ignore. If our friendship was going to continue— and especially if it was going to grow—it was time for us to be honest with each other.

Her voice over the radio snapped me out of my thoughts. Burles had taken all long-range communications away from us, but he couldn't do anything about the suit radios.

"I'm at the hatch, Captain. Boy, I sure wish you could cool these engines a bit." I wished so, too, but I didn't say anything. We both knew there was nothing I could do. "All right," she went on after a minute or two, "I've got the hatch open. Let's see, now . . ." Her voice trailed off and I found myself growing tense, waiting to hear what she found.

Nearly five minutes went by before she spoke again, five very long minutes. Then, "It's no good, Tom. I can see the widget. It appears to be a computer, for what that's worth. It means that we're probably following a pre-planned program rather than receiving signals from somewhere else. I can't remove it, though. He's sealed it in place, and I don't have any tools that can break the seal."

I sighed. Not very productive, I knew, but there didn't seem to be much else to do. "All right, Mikey," I said, "can we disable the computer? I'd rather fly on manual than let Burles be our pilot."

She was silent for a moment, looking it over. "No," she said eventually. "I don't think that would do any good. He's got feeder lines into the nav system. My guess is shutting down the computer won't return control of the ship to you."

I shook my head, not really surprised. "All right, Navigator. You might as well close up and come back inside."

She didn't respond for a few seconds, and when she did her voice was rather hesitant, something I hadn't heard from her before. "Um, Captain, if you don't mind, I'd prefer to stay out here. I don't know what Burles has in mind for you, sir, but I know what he wants to do with me. This isn't much of a hiding place, but if he doesn't know I'm even on board . . ."

I nodded. "Good idea, Mikey. All right, stay out there, but be careful. I'm not flying this thing. If you get separated from the ship, there's nothing I can do."

"Acknowledged, Captain." Then, in a faint voice, she added, "Though that might almost be better than Burles."

I didn't say anything. There was nothing to say, but I clenched my hands into fists and vowed that, no matter what I had to do, I would keep her safe from Burles.

Chapter Thirty-Five

The station didn't look any different than it had yesterday. No lights shone from its windows; no ships hovered near its docking bays. I was pretty sure all that was merely an illusion, however. It didn't make sense for Burles to send us to this station if he wasn't going to be there to greet us.

On the other hand, I realized, it was possible that we'd taken off sooner than he'd expected. Maybe, just maybe, we were going to get there before him.

It wasn't much of a hope, but I clung to it. It was better than nothing.

The docking maneuver made me sweat. I had piloted us through this very same routine just yesterday, and I remembered how tricky it had been. The thought of Burles—or anyone—trying to program that precise series of moves into a little box back on Brighthome made me very worried indeed.

As it turned out, my fears were misplaced.

When we were about a hundred meters out, my board suddenly lit up. I'd never seen this happen before, but a quick glance showed me what had happened: we had just interfaced with the station's computer. It was going to bring us in to dock.

In a way, that made me feel better, if only because it meant that we probably weren't going to crash into the side of the station. On the other hand, it meant that my hopes of beating Burles here had no chance of coming true.

My hands were still formed into fists and I forced myself to relax. Trying to find something to occupy myself with for the remaining few minutes, I covered the scanner controls back up. With Jamie in his camp, there was little chance that Burles didn't know we'd found out about them, but I covered them anyway, just in case. I didn't have any plan in mind; in fact, I was motivated more by spite than anything. If Burles didn't know about them, I didn't want him to find out from us.

After that, there was nothing for me to do, and no time left to do it in. Looking out through my screens, I watched us glide smoothly into position. I didn't think I'd ever have the chance to fly again, but still I found myself making mental notes of how the computer had brought us in.

Then I heard the faint snick of the docking collar mating with the side of our ship, and suddenly I had no thoughts for anything else. I turned to face the hatch, wishing for a weapon, anything that would allow me some control over what happened next. There was nothing, of course, and all

I could do was watch helplessly for the first sign of Burles.

But it wasn't Burles who came through that airlock. It was Jamie, a blaster held tightly in his hand.

Chapter Thirty-Six

"Jamie!" I cried, leaping up from my seat.

His face didn't light up at all at the sight of me, and his blaster didn't waver. "Sit down, Tom," he said, with no trace of warmth in his voice.

I sank back into my seat, a puzzled look on my face. What was with him? Was he being observed, maybe? Were his new shipmates testing him? I didn't know, but I decided to play along, at least for a while.

"What are you doing here?" he asked, leaning against the wall opposite me. His blaster remained pointed in my general direction.

I smiled slightly. "C'mon, Jamie. You left me that message. You didn't really think I could stay behind after reading it, did you?"

His own lips twitched slightly. They didn't make it to a full-blown smile, but I took it as a good sign. "Yeah. Hey, don't mention that message, okay?

Burles would be very unhappy if he knew I'd left it."

I had to grin at that. Here he was, a blaster pointed at me—even though we both knew he could never fire it—and he was asking favors. Still, "You got it, buddy," I said.

He smiled, too, for a moment. Then it faded, and he turned serious once again. "Where's Mikey, Tom?" he asked. "I hate to ask, but Burles is waiting for her."

I frowned. "That's twice now that you've mentioned him. Is he running things around here?"

Jamie shrugged. "As far as I know. Now where is she, Tom?"

I gave him a level look, trying to figure out how to handle this. I'd been prepared to answer to Burles, not to Jamie, and wasn't quite sure what to do. In the end, I looked once more at that blaster, still pointed in my general direction, and said, "She's back on Brighthome, of course. Where else?"

Jamie frowned. "Come on, Tom. I know better than that. What's more, I know her, too. Do you expect me to believe that she'd stay behind if she knew about this?"

"Jamie," and I put a slight edge in my voice, "I saw Burles working on our shuttle before I found your message. Now, tell me, since you know me so well: do you really think I'd let Mikey come on board a ship that Burles had had his hands in? I never told her about your message. That's all there is to it. And by the way, did you know that Burles was working on our ship?"

His eyes dropped at that, giving me my answer.

I sighed. "How long, Jamie? How long have you known?"

Slowly his eyes came back up to mine. He shrugged, but I could see the pain on his face. "A couple of months."

"Oh, Jamie," I said.

"Hey, I didn't think he'd do anything. Remember, he wasn't mad at either of us until a couple of days ago, when Mikey made him angry. And I did try to keep her off the ship, the one time she was on it."

I waved aside his last statement. "'When Mikey made him angry?'" I repeated. "My God, he's really got you snowed, doesn't he? You know what happened. The guy tried to rape her, and now you make it sound like it was her fault. Jamie, old buddy, what's come over you?"

He didn't answer that, of course. What could he say? He simply held my gaze for a moment before looking away. When his eyes came back to mine, I could see that this part of the conversation was over.

"So she's not here, huh?" he asked. "Burles is going to be mad, but I guess there's nothing I can do about it." He sighed, then gestured once with his blaster, "Come on, Tom."

"Come on? Where are we going?"

He blinked in surprise. "You didn't think you were going to get to stay on the ship, did you? No, Tom. Face it. You've seen this place; you know about the pirates. Their only choice now is to make you a pirate, too."

"But, Jamie, I don't want to be a pirate."

His face never changed. "I know that, Tom. Actually, I've known it for quite some time. It's really too bad that you decided to come after me. Now let's go. It's time to meet Burles."

He gestured again, and this time I rose and preceded him out the airlock. As we went, I couldn't help looking at that extensor tunnel, and wondering about it. I mean, it had completely sealed off the only entrance to the ship, and Mikey was on the other side. How was she going to get back in before her air ran out?

Maybe I should have been more worried about my own fate, but I couldn't get that thought out of my head.

You'll be all right, Mikey, I thought. *Somehow, I'll find a way to help you. I promise.*

Chapter Thirty-Seven

There were no signs of life as we walked the empty corridors of the space station. Everything was just as it had been when the three of us—Jamie, Mikey, and myself—had explored this place with the carefree abandon of happy children. Now, just two of us walked in the dimly-lit hallways, the thick carpeting underfoot muffling the sounds of our footsteps, but instead of exploring and having fun, my best friend had a blaster at my back.

After we'd gone a little ways, I couldn't take it any more.

"Are we being observed, Jamie? Do your friends have some kind of spy eyes watching us?"

He chuckled at that. "These guys? Tom, I doubt any of them have ever been here before—except for Burles. He's been here several times, meeting with the pirates, but I don't think even he's had much chance to explore the station. So, no, I don't think they've got spy-eyes on us. If there are any in the station, I doubt any of these guys know how to use them."

I stopped suddenly and turned on him. "Then put that thing away, will you?"

He chuckled again. "What? This thing?" And he waved his blaster at me. "You don't think this is a real weapon, do you? I mean, sure, it's a real blaster, but I don't think you've got anything to worry about. I doubt they'd trust me with one that's fully charged. You've got to remember, Tom: I haven't been with them very long. I don't think they trust me much more than they do you." He pointed the blaster at the floor and pressed the trigger.

He was wrong. The weapon was fully functional. Fortunately, he had it on its lowest setting. All it did was scorch the carpeting, but I was glad he'd pointed it at the floor. A moment later, after he'd quickly holstered it, he looked up at me, his face pale and drawn.

"Jeez, Tom," he said. "I'm sorry. I never figured—" But I could see that, beneath his shock, he was pleased as well, thinking that maybe they trusted him more than he'd thought. I didn't bother to disillusion him. Not yet, anyway. The way I figured it, they knew they didn't have much to worry about. One blaster wasn't going make much of a difference. I mean, we weren't going to take over the station with it, and it wasn't going to help me get my ship free, so why not let him have a functional weapon?

I waved his apology aside. He hadn't meant anything, I knew, and besides, something he'd said had struck me as more important.

"Jamie, how many pirates are there on this station right now?"

He didn't chuckle—he was still too shaken for that—but he did give me a faint smile. "Pirates? None, actually. Not yet, though Burles comes pretty close. The rest are kids like me, brought over from Brighthome to join up."

I nodded, thinking furiously. "And how many kids are there?"

He shrugged. "About ten. I didn't bother to count. Most of them are seniors, like us, but I think there are a couple of juniors, too. And Fritz."

That stopped me. "Fritz? They got him, too?"

Jamie nodded.

I sighed. "Poor kid." I'd hoped he'd be able to hold out against them. It was certain that he wasn't here by choice, but there was nothing I could do about it now. "And the pirates?" I asked. "When are they supposed to arrive?"

He shrugged again. "I'm not sure even Burles knows that. He just said we were supposed to wait here. He didn't say how long. Why?"

Which made it my turn to shrug. "No reason. I'm just fishing, I guess. Look," I went on, my voice low and serious, "Jamie, you've got to know that I'm not about to sign up with these guys. I don't want to be a pirate."

"You don't have any choice, Tom. The minute you decided to come after me, you were locked in."

I waved that off. "I don't agree. They can kidnap me. They can hold me here. But they can't make me do anything I don't want to do. The question is, old buddy, if an opportunity comes along for me, will you help me? I have to know."

There was pain in his eyes as he thought it over.

After several seconds, he said in a very soft voice, "I don't think so, Tom. I'm with them, now. You know that, if it came down to it, I couldn't make myself stop you, but I don't think I could help you, either."

I nodded and turned away, hiding the pain that I knew had to be showing on my face as well. We resumed walking, then, along the quiet, empty corridors.

After a few minutes, I brought up another subject. I didn't really want to talk to Jamie any more, at least not at that moment, but there were things I needed to know, and I wasn't sure I'd get another chance.

"So what should I expect from Burles?"

"I don't know, Tom. I know when we left he was pretty upset. He's really got a thing for Mikey, and when it looked like she was going to get away, well, he wasn't happy. Then we picked up the signal from your shuttle. That put him in a much better mood. Now, when he finds out she didn't come along— Let's just say I don't think he's going to like it."

"Good," I said. I started to say something more, but Jamie interrupted me.

"Sorry, Tom," he said, drawing his blaster once more. I noticed, however, that he was careful not to point it directly at me. "We're here." And he motioned toward the door directly in front of me. "This is the mess hall. It's where we've been holding our meetings, and this is where I was told to bring you."

I looked at him for a long moment. "It's still not too late, buddy. You and me, we could make a run for the ship. I bet you could figure out a way to get it to fly." I didn't want to tell him I knew about the widget Burles had installed because then he might start wondering *how* I knew. "We could get out of here, make it back to Brighthome, call the Space Guard, and spend the rest of our lives as heroes. What do you say?"

He didn't even look tempted. Only sad, and all he said was, "Open the door, Tom. Burles is waiting."

Well, I hadn't really expected him to go along with it. So why did I feel so disappointed?

I turned away, opened the door, and went inside to where Burles was waiting for me.

Chapter Thirty-Eight

He looked different, somehow. Bigger. Meaner. More confident.

He stood near a door in the far wall, facing me. His hands were on his hips, and he seemed to exude confidence and power.

I felt like I was seeing the real Burles for the first time, and I didn't like what I saw.

He was grinning as I walked through the door, but that grin changed to a frown as the door closed behind Jamie.

"Where is she?" he asked.

I assumed he was talking to me. At any rate, Jamie didn't rush to answer, so I said, "She's on Brighthome. She knows nothing of this."

Burles shifted his gaze to Jamie. "Is this true?"

Jamie took a step forward so that he stood next to me. On my right, I noticed, so that his blaster was on the far side of his body from me. "I believe so, sir," he said. "I searched Tom's ship and there was no sign of her."

"Too bad," Burles said. "Our ship is coming in out of the Orion sector, and isn't due in for six hours yet. I'd hoped to spend that time having a bit of fun. As it is . . ."

I didn't want to listen to that, so while they talked I took the opportunity to look around the room. It wasn't large—not nearly as big as it had seemed when there were just Jamie, Mikey, and me in it— and again I wondered about its history. Had this ever really been a mining station, or was it always used by pirates? At any rate, I saw half a dozen tables, and that was about it. Seated together at one of the tables were six kids I recognized from Brighthome. None of them were friends of mine, but I knew their faces. Fritz wasn't one of them.

Let's see, I thought. *Six here, plus Burles and Jamie, that's eight. Jamie thought there were ten, which means that Fritz and another pirate wannabe are somewhere on the station.* I didn't know what good that knowledge did me. I certainly didn't have anything even resembling a plan, but acting like there was some hope made me feel at least a little better.

Burles turned back to me abruptly and shattered my train of thought. "Why are you in your space suit?" he asked.

I shrugged. "As soon as I realized you were driving my ship, I figured I'd better take every precaution."

He grinned, and for a moment I thought I'd gotten away with smarting off. Then, without warning, he lashed out and backhanded me across the mouth. He'd done it casually, giving the impression that he'd only used a fraction of his strength, but the blow knocked me backwards and brought blood to my lips.

"Funny guy," he said. "I've been wondering what use to make of you. Now I know. You can be my court jester."

"Burles," surprisingly, it was Jamie who spoke up, "sir, you might not want to be too rough on him. They say he's pirate kin."

I had never been so glad for that rumor as I was at that moment. If it saved me from getting hit again, I would bless the guy who first came up with it.

But Burles only laughed. "Oh, yeah," he said, turning to address the other wannabes. "I've heard that story, but I've never believed it. In fact, I think just the opposite is true. I think Jenkins here is about the only person on Brighthome who *doesn't* want to be a pirate." He turned back to me. "How about it, Jenkins?" he said. "I'll tell you what. You tell me, right here and right now, that you've always wanted to be a pirate, and you can join up as an equal member of the crew. If not, well, hey, as I'm sure Jamie told you, you're a pirate anyway, but your rank will be somewhat lower.

"So what's the word, Jenkins? You want to be a member of my crew?"

I stood up straight and looked him straight in the eye. I knew I was going to pay for this, but as long as he was thinking about me and not about Mikey, her chances were that much better.

"I want," I said, drawing the back of my hand across my mouth to wipe away the blood, "you to go straight to hell."

He laughed again, and turned away to face the

rest of his crew to see how they were reacting. Then he spun back toward me, his hand lashing out in another vicious blow. I saw it coming, of course. I'd seen it coming even before I spoke, but I couldn't get out of the way. He was too fast, and I had no experience at fighting.

This time, he knocked me sprawling, and I thought I felt a couple of teeth loosen in my jaw. Still, I got back to my feet, my hands forming themselves into fists at my side, and took a step forward.

He grinned at me. "You want to try it, Jenkins? I've got to admit, you'll never get a better chance. All right, I'll make you another proposition: we'll fight, if you want, and if you win, I'll turn your ship back over to you and let you go. Now I can't be any fairer than that, can I? So what do you say? No, don't bother to answer. Just go ahead and take your best shot."

I intended to. God knows I wanted to, even though I knew what would happen. I'd have given anything right then for the ability to wipe that smug smile off his face, but I knew I had no chance against him. Still, I was about to take another step forward, my fists rising in front of me, when the door behind me flew open and another wannabe burst into the room.

"Sir!" he said. "Station radar has picked up a series of modified pulses originating from within the station!"

"What?"

I recognized the kid from my physics class. His name was Bob. Something of a quiet guy. I wouldn't have expected to find him among the pirates. I guess you just never know who the dreamers are, or what their dreams might be.

Which meant, I realized, that either Jamie was wrong in his count, or Fritz was out there in the station by himself, and I doubted that. He'd joined their group too reluctantly. Which meant Jamie's count was wrong. I couldn't see how that information would help me, but I filed it away anyway. Just in case.

Bob said, "As near as we can tell, the pulses are coming from somewhere in the outer docking ring."

Burles froze at that, then slowly turned toward me, his face a frozen mask of rage. "Tell me, Jenkins, does your ship have modified pulse radar capability?"

I didn't answer him, though. I was too busy trying to figure out what it meant.

"Yes, sir." It was Jamie who spoke up for me. "Hyperwave, too."

"And you didn't tell me this?" Burles struck out again, and this time it was Jamie who stumbled back, a cry bursting from his lips.

I started to take that final step forward that would bring me within range of Burles, but he spun back toward me, his hands clenched tightly in front of him. "So she stayed on Brighthome, did she? Then who, I wonder, is using your radar?" He didn't wait for an answer. Spinning back toward his crew of wannabes, he started barking out orders. "Bob, get back to your post. Watch for any sign that anybody's picked up these pulses. We don't want the Guard getting curious, but if they do I'd better know about it. Martin, Loren," he indicated two out of the group seated at the table, "get down to that ship and restrain whoever's on board. Watch out, though. She knows some tricks, so keep your blasters out and your guards up. Got it? Then get going!"

Turning back to Jamie, who was just now picking himself up off the ground, he asked, "Any thoughts on this?"

Jamie glared at him, but he answered quickly enough. "Just one, sir: I think you're right. I think she's trying to draw the attention of that Spacer Guard ship I told you about. The *Daedalus*."

Burles nodded. "Yeah, kid, the question is, will they do anything about it?"

Jamie shrugged. "Modified pulse radar signals coming from an unidentified source in a system where the pirates are rumored to hang out? Yes, sir. I'd think they would check it out."

Burles nodded again. "I think you're right. All right," he turned back to the four remaining at the table. "Steve, John, remove the controlling device from that ship and prepare to take it out of dock. If the Guard shows up, you're just a couple of kids from Brighthome out joyriding, and you stumbled across the scanner controls. You were just playing with them, and you're sorry for causing any alarm. Got it? Then get going, but remember—don't leave dock unless there's some sign of the Guard. And as for you two," he picked out the remaining wannabes, "get moving. I want this station shut down tight. We're not putting out any radio signals, so that's no problem, but I want any and all signs of habitation shielded or removed. Got it? I don't want the Guard coming here to check us out, but if they do, I don't want them to find anything."

There was a brief bustle of activity. A moment later, just the three of us—Burles, Jamie, and myself—were left in the mess hall.

"Jamie," Burles said. The note of authority had left his voice. Now it was just low and mean. "Jamie,

I don't like surprises. You've given me a couple of nasty ones now. Don't give me any more."

Beside me, Jamie only nodded.

"And as for you, Jenkins—"

I tensed for another blow, but none came. Instead, he said, "This station has been a good deal for us. If we have to lose it because of you— Well, let's just say you won't be any happier than we are."

He was blaming me, obviously, and I didn't really mind. I only wish I felt I'd done something to earn his anger. So far, though, it had been all Mikey.

Thinking of her, I glanced down at the space suit I was still wearing. I could feel the weight of the helmet tugging at the back of my collar, and I knew that the radio was still open. If I could only figure out a way to pull the helmet on without making Burles suspicious, I could listen in and find out whether Mikey got away or not. I didn't dare let Burles see me do it, though. If he started thinking about those radios, he might figure out what Mikey had done, just as I thought I'd figured it out. I didn't want that, so I had to content myself with hoping she got away.

We'd all know soon enough, anyway, when Martin and Loren reported back—empty-handed, or with Mikey at blasterpoint.

This would have been a good time to try and overpower Burles. He had a blaster strapped to his waist—just like all the other pirate wannabes did— but so far he hadn't shown any inclination to reach for it. His first impulse, as always, seemed to be to use his fists. Now, with all his underlings out of the room, it would have been the perfect opportunity for Jamie to draw his own weapon and turn the tables on Burles.

One look at my best friend, however, told me that it wouldn't happen. He still had a rather sullen look to him, and it was obvious that his jaw was sore, but he wouldn't meet my gaze. He knew what I was thinking, I was certain, and didn't want any part of it.

I kept trying to catch his eye, however, and when, after another minute or two, I succeeded, he gave me a small, almost imperceptible shake of his head. I frowned, but I wasn't surprised. He'd seen some of the harsh realities of pirate life, perhaps, but not enough to disillusion him entirely.

Reluctantly, I put my hopes aside. Even distracted, Burles was more than I could deal with alone.

Stifling a sigh, I settled in to wait.

Chapter Thirty-Nine

"Burles," I said a few minutes later. "There's one thing I don't understand." I'd decided to try talking to him for a couple of reasons: one, I wanted to keep him from thinking too much about Mikey and what she'd been doing with the radar; and, two, there really was something I wanted to know.

He'd been pacing when I broke the silence. At my words, he turned to face me, an arrogant smile on his face. "Only one thing, Jenkins? I'm amazed."

I refused to be baited, though. Instead, I merely nodded and said, "Yeah. How did you meet the pirates?" I was thinking on my feet, trying to come up with something to keep him distracted. "I mean, it just doesn't make sense that it was by accident, and yet you never earned your flames, so you were never off Brighthome—or at least, you weren't off Brighthome often, or for long. No, the way I figure it, there must be someone at the Youth Center, someone who is either a pirate or who is at least connected to the pirates. Some sort of recruiter, I guess. The way I figure it, he'd have to know most of the kids, and he'd have to be able to leave Brighthome frequently without raising any suspicion. The thing is, I can't think of anyone who fits that description, so tell me: who was your contact at the Center?"

His smile hadn't slipped at all, but as I finished he made a mocking sort of bow in my direction. "Well, what do you know?" he said. "A pilot with some brains. I think the pirates will be very pleased with me for bringing you to them—once we've gotten your attitude readjusted. As for your theory, you're right and you're wrong. There is a contact person on Brighthome—a 'recruiter,' if you will—but that's as much as you got right. He doesn't have to know most of the kids, you see. He only has to know a few. They can tell him about the others; they can find the best choices and talk them into signing up. And he doesn't have to leave Brighthome very often, either. Radio would be too obvious, but there are lots of other ways to smuggle messages in and out. It happens all the time."

I nodded at that. "All right, I can see that, but you still haven't answered my question: who is it?"

I was pressing, hoping that Mikey would be listening—assuming she'd gotten away, of course—and that she'd be able to do something with this information.

Burles' grin widened, and I had the distinct impression that he wasn't going to answer me. Before he could commit himself, I rushed on, "Unless, of course, you don't want to tell me," I said. "If you think I might escape, I can see where you wouldn't want me to know."

As I'd hoped, his grin grew even wider. "Escape? No, Jenkins, I don't think you might escape. All right, since you're so interested, and since I know the information will never get out, I'll tell you. Why not?"

But he never got the chance. At that moment, the door opened, and Martin walked in, beaming from ear to ear. My heart sank at the interruption, but it sank even lower when I realized why Martin seemed so happy: trailing at his heels, Loren two steps behind her with his blaster drawn, was Mikey.

Burles chuckled, a very self-satisfied sound, and if he'd been within reach I would have hit him. As it was, I could only clench my fists helplessly and watch.

She didn't look any different, except that her helmet was no longer sealed. Instead, like mine, it was hanging from the back of her collar. Her head was high, and there was defiance in her eyes, but I noticed she wouldn't meet my gaze as they led her past me. When they were about five feet in front of Burles, they stopped, and then Loren and Martin both withdrew back to the table where I'd first seen them.

Burles met her with his hands on his hips, and that same cocky, infuriating smile on his face.

"Well, well, well," he said, running his eyes insolently up and down her body. "Welcome to Freebooter Station, my dear."

She didn't say anything. She just crossed her arms in front of her and watched him.

If anything, his smile grew slightly at her attitude.

"Now, is that any way to act, my dear?" he said. "Especially when I have this?" And he drew his blaster, the first time I'd seen him even touch it.

"Go ahead," she said, her voice firm and strong. "Kill me. I'd rather be dead than feel your hands on me."

"Oh, no," he said, taking two steps forward. That put him just outside her reach, and I suspected he knew that. "You don't understand. I'm not threatening *you*, my dear. Oh, no. Quite the contrary. I'm threatening *him*." And he raised his blaster and pointed it straight at me. "You will cooperate with me, Mikey. You will make me happy, or he will die."

I couldn't see Mikey's face, but I could see how her shoulders sagged in sudden defeat.

"No, Mikey," I said. "Don't worry about me. Don't give in to him."

Burles only laughed. Then, without warning, he took another step forward, reached out, and grabbed the front of Mikey's space suit. I saw her arms come up reflexively, but she didn't strike him. In fact, she didn't do anything as he pulled out a knife and cut away the entire front of her space suit.

"Very good," he said to her. My own face was burning with shame and an impotent rage as he reached out and tugged slightly at the zipper of her jump suit. "Now," he said, speaking softly, but very confidently, "you and I are going to go through that little door over there. It's another little dining room—I believe it's where the officers ate—and I think we'll find it quite comfortable." Holstering his weapon, he looked over at Jamie and said, "Draw your blaster, kid, and if I come out that door with anything less than a smile on my face, kill him."

Jamie did as instructed, stepping behind me and

putting the muzzle of his weapon in the small of my back. I didn't believe he would shoot me, but even so there was nothing I could do as Burles led Mikey away, that same, sickening smile plastered on his face.

"Oh, Mikey," I whispered. "Mikey, I'm so sorry."

And then the door slid shut behind them.

Chapter Forty

"Jamie," I said, the moment the door was closed, "Jamie, you can't let this happen." I was speaking softly, not wanting to alert Loren and Martin. They were talking among themselves, giggling and laughing, and I wasn't too worried about them, but I kept my voice low just to be sure.

"There's nothing I can do about it, Tom," Jamie said, in a whisper even softer than mine.

"Sure there is, buddy. Look at those two. They're not paying any attention to us. We could get the drop on them, get their blasters, and then go in and stop Burles before he does anything to Mikey, but we have to move now. C'mon, Jamie. Are you with me?"

"Tom—"

"Dammit, Jamie," I hissed, "that's Mikey in there! Now, I'll tell you what: I'm going to go over to Loren and Martin. I know you won't shoot me, but

I'm not so certain about them. The question is, are you going to let them?"

I started to step forward but he reached out and grabbed the helmet hanging from the back of my collar. "But these are pirates, Tom! This is my chance!"

I turned, then, and looked at him, torn between the conflicting needs of my only two friends. "I know," I told him. "They offered you a home. I know how important that is to you, and I'm sorry to have to be the one to ruin it for you, but, Jamie, you saw how Burles treated you. Jeez, he hit you even harder than he hit me. What kind of a home is that, huh, buddy?"

His face fell at my words, and I felt bad for making him see even part of the ugly truth. At the moment, however, I didn't have much choice.

"Jamie, I'm sorry, but we're out of time. You saw Burles. I don't think he's got much patience, and I'm not going to let anything happen to Mikey. Now, are you with me?"

But he didn't answer. His face had gone pale, and I could see he was still thinking about what I'd said.

Sighing, I turned away and started heading over to where Loren and Martin were talking and laughing.

I got about halfway there before they noticed me. I saw them look at me, then look at Jamie, then look at each other. I got another few steps closer before Loren pulled his blaster.

"Stop right there, Jenkins," he commanded, but I thought I heard a quaver in his voice.

I shook my head, and continued to take slow, small steps forward. "I don't think so, Loren. You're not going to shoot me. You know it; I know it; heck, even Burles knew it. That's why he gave the job to Jamie, even knowing we were best friends." I saw the blaster waver, and I took another step. Three or four more and I'd be able to reach out and snatch the weapon.

Martin had gone as pale as Jamie. He sat there, his gaze bouncing back and forth between Loren and me, and never once reached for his own weapon.

They'd been a lot cockier back in the cafeteria, but that had been mild stuff. This was serious, and it was clear they didn't know how to handle it. Which was lucky for me, because I didn't know how to handle it, either.

"C'mon, Loren," I said, "we don't hang around much anymore. Just kind of grew apart, I guess, but we used to be friends." Which was true. A couple of years ago, back when he first came to Brighthome, we did a few things together. We never had a falling out, or anything. Just, as I told him, went our separate ways. "So, listen, for old time's sake, why don't you give me your weapon and let me stop Burles before he does anything."

Loren looked at me for a long moment before shaking his head. "No, Tom," he said. "You're right, I'm not going to shoot you, but I'm not going to give you my blaster, either." Saying that, he slipped it back into its holster and then nudged Martin with his elbow. "In fact, I'd say that Marty and I don't need to shoot you. I figure the two of us can hold you till Burles comes out. Now, it's up to you. Go back to where you were, or we knock you down and sit on you."

And that was when Jamie spoke up. "I don't think so, Loren."

I glanced over at him and saw that he had his weapon trained on the two of them. His face was calm, and I knew after one look that he'd overcome his earlier indecision. That must have been obvious to Loren and Martin, too, because they didn't try to stop me as I took the last few steps and relieved them of their blasters.

Crossing over to the door, I paused long enough to look back at my friend. "Thanks, Jamie," I said, and then I opened the door and leaped through it, praying I wasn't too late.

Chapter Forty-One

I didn't know what I expected to see when I went through that door. I had a lot of ideas in my mind—half-formed images that I refused to let develop into full-blown scenes. Whatever it was, though, that I expected to see, it certainly wasn't the sight that greeted me as I entered the officers' mess hall.

Mikey and Burles were both still on their feet, and they were standing several feet apart. Both were down in a fighter's crouch, and in the moment that we all stood frozen I could make out a couple of other details. Burles had a red mark on his left cheek and the beginnings of some puffiness around one of his eyes. *Good for you, Mikey*, I thought, and then I noticed that she, too, bore the marks of his fist high up on the right side of her face. I knew that mark. It was the sign of his back-handed blow. I had a couple just like it.

They had been facing each other, both of them

focused completely on what the other was doing, but my entrance spoiled that. Burles jerked his head toward me, and when he saw who it was that interrupted him, he dropped his hand to his blaster. I had just enough time to wonder if I could actually bring myself to fire the weapon in my hand, but before I could find out the chance was past.

Burles had turned to look at me. Mikey never did. She saw him turn his head and immediately she launched herself at him, leaping through the air and bringing the soles of her boots solidly against his jaw. His eyes rolled up in his head and he sagged to the floor.

Relief shot through me, but only for a moment. Mikey, her concentration completely focused on Burles, had never turned to see who was in the door. I hadn't given that a thought until I saw her use her momentum to leap forward, grab Burles' blaster, and start bringing it up toward me.

"Mikey!" I cried. "It's me! Don't shoot!"

I don't know if I needed to say that or not. I only know I couldn't help it. The words burst out of me as I saw that blaster start swinging in my direction. She checked herself, though, and a moment later we were in each other's arms, laughing and crying and simply holding each other.

She was the first one to speak. "What happened?" she asked. "How did you get free, and with a blaster, too?"

I told her, as quickly as I could, what had happened. She was happy that Jamie was back on our side, but she seemed somewhat distracted as I spoke, too.

"What is it?" I asked, when I had finished telling her my little saga.

She sighed, then, and dropped her gaze, and said the three words I'd least expected to hear. "I'm sorry, Tom," she said.

"Sorry?" I asked. "What for?"

She motioned toward Burles. "That. I came in here fully intending to let him do whatever he wanted. After all, your life was at stake, but when he put his hand on me—" Her voice trailed off into a shamed silence.

"Mikey," I said softly, reaching out to touch her unharmed cheek. "When I saw you go through that door, knowing what was about to happen and that I was the reason you would allow it, I wanted to die. I never want anything bad to happen to you, and I couldn't bear to be the cause of it. I'm glad you fought him off. I don't think I could have lived with myself, otherwise."

Slowly, her eyes came up to mine, and for a moment I thought I saw something warm shine within them. The she was herself again, hard and cocky.

"Come on," she said. "We've got work to do."

Chapter Forty-Two

She sobered quickly and went to stand over Burles. Looking down at him, her hair fell across her face so that I couldn't see her expression, but I felt I didn't really need to. I could see the way she kept fingering the blaster she'd taken from him.

"I could kill him now," she said, and even knowing what she'd been through, I was surprised at the venom in her voice.

"Yes," I said. "You could, but you'd be doing more harm to yourself than he ever could. I mean, you and I know that you'd be doing the galaxy a favor by killing him, but it would still be murder. Leave him for the Guard, Mikey."

She snorted at that, a harsh, twisted little laugh. "The Guard, eh, Tom?"

I ignored her reaction—I still wanted to talk to her about that, but this wasn't the time for it. I was just happy to see that all she did was reach down and take the holster from his belt and attach it to her own. Putting her weapon away, she looked up at me and said, "Well, Captain. What now?"

That was a good question. Not having really expected to succeed, I hadn't made any plans. I didn't really know what to do next.

I pointed at Burles. "How long will he be out?"

She shrugged. "It's hard to say. Most people would probably be unconscious for an hour, but with him I don't know. Everyone's different. Sometimes the big guys come around quicker, sometimes they stay out longer than you'd expect."

I nodded, thinking.

"I could always hit him again," she said, fingering the grip of her blaster.

"No, Mikey," I said, before I realized she was kidding. We shared a grin, and then I said, "All right, the way I see it, we should just get our ship and get out of here. Jamie said there are about ten pirate wannabes on this station. We've got Burles here, and he's got two more out in the other room, but that still leaves seven, and I suspect there are one or two more. I'm afraid that if we try anything too brave, we'll just end up getting captured again, and the next time I don't think we'll be so lucky."

"Should we find some rope and tie them up?"

I shook my head. "I don't think so. In the first place, we didn't find any yesterday when we searched this place. If there is any here, we could waste a lot of time finding it. In the second place, someone could come in at any time and find them. No, like I said, I think we should just go. There are a couple of kids on our ship, but I think we can take them, and the good thing is that they should have removed Burles' little control device by now. On the other hand, I'm not pulling rank, here. If you've got a better idea, I want to hear it."

She shook her head. "I'm with you, Captain." As she spoke, she peeled off the remains of her tattered space suit and tossed it, helmet and all, at Burles' feet. "There, you bastard," she said. "Sleep with that."

"All right," I said when she was ready. "Let's get Jamie and get out of here."

Not much had changed in the outer room. Loren and Martin were still talking among themselves, but they were no longer laughing. Jamie was about ten feet away from them—close enough that he could see everything they did, but far enough that they couldn't rush him—but he'd moved slightly so he could watch both doors, too. When we came out of the officers' mess, his blaster started to swing toward us, but he stopped as soon as he recognized us and a big smile broke out across his face.

"Mikey," he said, "are you all right?"

"Yeah, Jamie," she said. "I'm fine."

His gaze dropped for a moment. "I'm sorry I wasn't more help."

She waved that off. "Hey, you came through in the end, and that's what counts."

I hated to break up their little reunion, but I had suddenly become very much aware of the time. So many things could still go wrong: Burles could wake up early; some of the other kids could come in, enough of them to give us problems; the Space Guard could come by and force the kids on our ship to take off, leaving us trapped on this station.

So many things, and those were just the first things that came to mind.

"Come on," I said. "Loren, Martin, I want you to go into that little dining room with Burles. He's unconscious, but beyond that he's all right. I don't think you should try and wake him up for a while. When he does wake up, you know he'll come after us, and if he does while we're still on the station we'll have to kill him." I didn't know if they'd believe me or not, but it was worth a shot.

We took their holsters so I could have one, which left us with four complete sets. That was all right, though. The way things were going, I had the feeling we couldn't have too many weapons.

Reluctantly, the two of them filed into the officers' mess, and Mikey used her blaster to seal the door. It wasn't a very good seal, nothing like a real weld, but it was the best we could do, and we hoped it would slow them down a little.

Then, having done all we could, we headed off toward our ship.

Chapter Forty-Three

"So, Mikey," I said as we trotted along the carpeted hallways. It was funny how the place didn't seem so empty now. "You never did tell me how you got into the station."

She shrugged, as if to say it was nothing much, but then she gave me a lopsided grin. "It was nothing much," she said. "After we docked, and after I heard Jamie take you off the ship, I went exploring. I figured there had to be some other means into the station, if only for workers to do repairs and things, and I was right. I found a maintenance hatch not too far from the ship and used it to get inside. After that, it was simply a matter of finding my way back to the ship and listening to what was happening to you."

"Yeah," Jamie said, "I wanted to ask you about that. You could have stayed on the *Hobo One* for a long time if you hadn't used the radar. What was the point of that? All you did was give yourself away."

"No, Jamie," I said. "That's not all she did." I was gratified to catch a surprised look on Mikey's face when I said that. "If I'm right, what she did was use the radar to send a coded message to the *Daedalus*, informing the Guard of the incoming pirate ship. Am I right, Mikey?"

She grinned at me. "You're right, Captain. Which, unfortunately, means that the *Daedalus* is on its way to intercept the real pirates, and not coming here to help us out."

I hadn't thought about that.

"All right," I said. "We're on our own. Let's get our ship back and get out of here." And then I stopped.

"What is it?" Mikey asked.

"Fritz," I said. "He's here, and I'm certain he doesn't want to be. We've got to find a way to take him with us."

Mikey's face had gone hard as soon as I started talking, but it was Jamie who answered me.

"No, Tom," he said.

"No?" I said. "What do you mean?"

"He's here by choice," Jamie said.

"But—"

"No buts. You're right in that Burles put a lot of pressure on him, but in the end he signed up of his own free will. I know him, Tom. We used to hang out together, back before you and I became friends. He sees things pretty much the same way I did. It may have started with intimidation, but now he truly believes his future lies with the pirates."

I nodded at that. It made our job just a little bit

easier, but still I felt disappointed, as though I'd failed at something important.

And I had, I realized. I should have found a way to help him before it had gone this far.

"Come on," I said, putting that out of my mind for the moment. "Let's get to the ship."

After everything else, the reclaiming of the *Hobo One* went surprisingly smoothly. Steve and John were the two wannabes manning the controls, and they weren't expecting any trouble. We just walked in, waved our blasters, and that was it.

I suspected things would have been a lot different if we'd been going up against real pirates.

"Jamie, get their weapons and their holsters," I said. "I don't know if they have spare blasters or not, but maybe by taking their holsters, too, we can make things a little harder on them."

He did as I asked. "You know, Tom," he said after relieving them of their gear, "we've got six of their weapons, now. If they each had only one, that leaves them with four, which means we outgun them. You want to try to take the entire station?"

I didn't have to think that one over for long. "No, Jamie, though it's a good idea. For one thing, we don't know if they have any spares. For another, we don't know where all the kids are. We know Bob and at least one other, and maybe Fritz, too, are in the control room—which reminds me, they're going to know as soon as we pull out; let's hope they can't do anything about it—but there's another pair out 'securing the station.' We have no idea where they are. All it would take was for them to learn what was going on and we'd be in trouble."

He nodded at that, and I turned to Mikey. She seemed unhappy, but she didn't say anything. "Why don't you check and see if one of these two has that device Burles had installed in the engine compartment? You're the only one who's seen it, so you're the only one who can recognize it."

It only took her a moment. John had it in the breast pocket of his jumpsuit. Looking at it, it was hard to believe that something so small had caused so much trouble.

"All right," I said. "Now what? Anybody have any ideas what to do with them?"

"Shoot them," Jamie said. I was glad he said that. I knew he was kidding, but they didn't, and maybe that threat would help keep them in line.

"Maybe," I said. "Let's see if we can come up with something else, first."

"Let's space them," Mikey said. "Get them into suits, and then put them out the airlock as soon as we pull away. If we give them a good push, they should be able to reach the station. It may take them a while, but eventually they'll find a hatch and get back in."

That one I had to think over. It was a good idea, but in the end I rejected it. "No," I said. "I don't think so. It would take too long. Once we pull away, I want to turn this baby on its tail and jet out of here."

Jamie and Mikey both nodded at that. Turning to the two would-be pirates, I said, "We're going to let you go, but there's something I want you to think about. We're not going to be recaptured easily. Right now, all we want is to get away. If you raise the alarm and Burles figures out a way to bring us back, we're going to come in shooting, and you'll be at the top of our target list. So, it's up to you, but I think you might want to be a little careful."

I didn't wait for their reaction. I simply nodded to Jamie and he put them out through the airlock. He stayed there, his hand on the release lever, while Mikey and I took our positions.

"Everything's powered up," I said, raking my eyes across the panel.

"How can that be?" Mikey asked. "I thought this ship was keyed to you."

I nodded. "You're right, but don't forget about Burles' little device. After we docked here, I didn't bother to power it down. I didn't see the need, and I'm not sure I could have, anyway." I looked down at my controls again. "Give me a course back to Brighthome, fastest route. Unless, of course, you want to meet up with the *Daedalus*?"

She turned a startled look my way, but I kept my head down, only looking at her out of the corner of my eye.

"No," she said slowly, "Brighthome's fine. There may be a battle between the *Daedalus* and the pirate ship, and I don't think we want to take this runabout into that."

I nodded. As soon as I'd received the course from her, I turned back to Jamie. "Release extensor tunnel," I said.

He pulled the lever. "We're free," he said a moment later, his eyes on the readout by the hatch.

This time I didn't worry about my flames. I turned the ship as quickly as I could, brought her in line with the course Mikey had given me, and hit the jets.

A moment later, the station was receding behind us, with no sign of pursuit.

"My friends," I said, leaning back in my chair, "I think we're home free."

Chapter Forty-Four

Five minutes into our flight, Mikey turned to me and said, "Request permission to use the scanners."

"Granted," I said, "though I'd like to know why."

She uncovered the controls and busied herself with them as she answered, "I'd like to know if the *Daedalus* has made contact with the pirates or not. I may not be able to tell for sure with this, but I'd like to try."

I nodded. "Of course." I should have figured that out for myself. "The radio's working now," I said. "Would you like to send a message to the *Daedalus*?"

She shook her head. "No, sir. If they haven't made contact with the pirates yet, I don't want to give away their presence." She glanced at her board, made a couple of adjustments, and then shook her head. "I can't be sure, but it doesn't look like the pirates have made it into the system yet."

A thought occurred to me then. "Can Burles warn them away? I mean, I think it's a safe bet that the station has a comm system."

I felt like a fool for not having thought of that earlier. Fortunately, Mikey shook her head.

"I don't think we have to worry about that," she said. "Yes, Burles could warn them off, but the Guard will be watching for that. Even if the pirates don't respond, if they just receive the message and try to run, the *Daedalus* will be able to track them. Once they've got a lock on them, the pirate ship won't get away."

"Good," I said. "Then we've only got one thing to worry about."

"What's that?" she asked.

"The pirate on Brighthome. If Burles told him about the device on our ship, he's going to be awfully suspicious when we show up back at the Youth Center. I just wish we knew who he was."

"Yeah," Mikey said. "I'm sorry about that. I had already sent the message before you got Burles talking about that. It was rotten timing, but by then there wasn't anything I could do about it."

"Hey," I said. "Don't be sorry about anything. I didn't mean to make it sound like you goofed up. Jeez, Mikey, what you did was unbelievably brave. You've got nothing to feel bad about."

"Right." That was the first word Jamie had spoken since we'd left the station. I'd just figured he was feeling bad about his role in things, and I'd wanted to give him time to work through it. I was glad to see he was starting to take part in things again.

"Say, Jamie," I said, turning to look at him, "you wouldn't happen to have any idea who Burles was talking about, would you?"

"No, Tom. I don't think Burles let anyone know. Most of us didn't even know there was a real pirate on Brighthome."

I nodded. That was pretty much what I'd expected. If I was the pirate there, I'd be very careful how many high school kids knew about me. It would be too easy for someone to let something slip.

"Well, let's think it through," Mikey said. "You two know Brighthome better than I. Who would you suspect?"

"It would almost have to be one of the teachers, wouldn't it?" Jamie asked.

I shook my head. "Not really. You heard what Burles said. Whoever it is, he only has to make contact with some of the kids. The grapevine does the rest."

"Yeah," Jamie said, "but we have to start somewhere. Let's look at the teachers, first."

I shrugged and thought about it. It didn't take long. "There's only one choice," I said. "Most of the teachers are too old and fat and lazy to be pirates. All they want is to put in their time, avoid trouble, and cash their checks."

"Unless one of them is acting," Mikey said.

I shook my head. "I don't believe it. No one's that good an actor."

She smiled. "Who, then? You said there was only one choice."

Jamie answered before I could. "Mr. Forrester," he said. "He's tough. He'd make a good pirate, and his short hair would be perfect inside a space helmet."

I nodded. "Of the teachers, Mr. Forrester gets my vote. But I think there's a better suspect, don't you, Mikey?"

She nodded. "Mr. Pierson."

"What are you talking about?" Jamie asked. I hadn't had a chance to tell him about our little meeting with the administrator.

"He's on the take," I said. "When Mikey came to him with some problems, he flat out told her she'd have to bribe him to help. Which," I added, "was probably a mistake."

Mikey simply nodded.

Jamie started to say something else when Mikey's voice suddenly cut across our conversation. "Hyperwave's picking up a ship, Captain."

"The *Daedalus*?" I asked.

"No, sir. It's coming from the station."

"Course?"

She made a couple of adjustments, and when she looked up at me her face had gone pale. "It's coming our way."

"Burles," I said. "On our tail and coming for blood." I looked down at my own controls, but there wasn't much more I could do. We were already at maximum acceleration.

"You should have let me kill him when we had the chance," Mikey said.

I couldn't tell if she was kidding or not, so all I said was, "Yeah." Then, "All right. We know he's on a shuttle like this one; we saw the empty bay in the hangar. Jamie, on the flight over, did you see any indication that it had been modified at all, souped up or given weapons or anything like that?"

He shook his head. "Not that I saw."

"Good." I glanced at my board again. "We'll touch down in approximately eight minutes. Mikey, what is he, about five minutes behind us?" She nodded.

"Okay, then it's decision time, my friends. What do we do when we hit Brighthome? Any suggestions?"

"Well," Mikey was the first to speak, "we can't go to anyone for help. Without knowing who the pirate is—and especially if it *is* Mr. Pierson—we might end up running straight to him."

"Agreed. What about you, Jamie? Any thoughts?"

"Yeah," he said. "There are three of us, and only one of him. On top of that, we're armed. Why don't we simply wait for him to land, and then get the drop on him?"

"I don't like it," I said. "For one thing, we don't know that there's only one of him. He could have all eight of the wannabes with him, and though they might not be any great shakes in a fight, they probably won't be any worse than we are. Besides, we don't know that he's going to come in at the same place we are. For all we know, he'll land at the old mining settlement, and then come for us at his leisure. I'd like to have a plan that gives us some control over where he finds us."

"In that case," Jamie said, "I suggest the caves."

"The caves?" Mikey asked. "Why there?"

"For one thing, it's our turf. We know it better than he does. For another, I don't believe he can reach us there."

"Why not?" I asked.

"Think about it, Tom. You remember the squeeze just before the tunnel opens up? You can barely fit through there, and Burles is bigger than you. I don't think he could make it, but even if he does, we'll be sitting just beyond, with our blasters in our hands. He wouldn't have a chance."

"That goes both ways," Mikey said. "After all, if he can't come in without getting blasted, then we might not be able to come out for the same reason. We could be trapped there for quite some time."

I answered that one for Jamie. "Not for all that long, actually. That is, assuming that the *Daedalus* will come looking for us. What do you think, Mikey? Can we expect some backup from them after they deal with the pirates?"

Again she gave me a long look before answering, but eventually she nodded. "Good," I said. "Do you see anything else wrong with it?"

She thought it over for a minute, then shook her head. "Actually, no. I think it's a good idea."

"All right," I said. "That's it, then. We head for the caves as soon as we touch down."

There was silence for a moment, and then Mikey suddenly turned toward her scanner controls. "Burles is sending a message," she said.

"To the pirates?"

"No, sir. It's aimed at Brighthome."

"Brighthome? All right, we can bet he's contacting the pirate there, but what in the world is he saying?"

I couldn't figure it out.

"It's a short message, sir," Mikey added. "I'm not familiar with this code, but it couldn't be more than a few words."

Which didn't really tell me much.

Burles, I thought. *What are you up to, Burles?*

But I had no answers for that, and I turned my attention back to my controls.

Chapter Forty-Five

We didn't have any trouble with the landing. In fact, I was kind of glad that Frank wasn't there to take the ship off my hands. I wasn't looking forward to explaining why I'd taken it out without authorization.

We grabbed all the blasters, sealed the ship, and headed for the caves on the run. I didn't think Burles would come looking there right away, but I didn't want to take chances. I wanted plenty of time to get ready before he showed up.

Walking into the outer cave was like coming home. I'd always liked the place, but I never expected to feel quite so good about it. After that station, though, I felt like I could be happy staying there for the rest of my life.

"Jamie," I said, "I hate to ask you this, but—"

"You want me to keep watch out here," he said.

"Yeah. You're the smallest of us. That squeeze at the end of the tunnel hardly slows you down. Stick around here, will you, and let us know if Burles shows up?"

"You got it," he said.

I nodded my thanks and Mikey and I withdrew to the campsite.

"You think he'll find this place?" Mikey asked me after we'd gotten settled.

"Yeah, I think so," I said. "It's common knowledge that Jamie and I hang out here a lot. I think, after he checks the rest of the Center and doesn't find us, he'll come here. I just hope that it takes him long enough that the *Daedalus* gets here first."

She nodded. "You know the thing that bugs me? I can't get that message out of my mind, the one he sent from his ship."

"You mean who he sent it to?"

"Well, yes, I guess so, but even more than that, I can't help thinking that the timing was no coincidence. He sent it just after we made our plans."

"True," I said, "and if there was anyway he could have known them, I'd be worried, too. But how could he?"

She nodded, but didn't seem convinced. Considering what she had to fear from Burles, I couldn't really blame her for that.

"Well," I said, "I'm going to lie down for a while. It's been a long day. Go ahead and use Jamie's bedroll if you want. He won't mind."

I didn't think I'd be able to sleep, not with the possibility of Burles showing up, but I wanted to rest. I didn't get to. I started to lay back, and that's when I noticed the space suit helmet still attached to my collar. The thing was so light, and we'd all been so distracted, that I simply forgot all about it.

"Um, Mikey?"

"Yes." She had started over toward Jamie's bedroll, but she froze at the ominous note in my voice.

"You know how I said Burles couldn't have known our plans?"

"Yeah."

"You left your helmet with him, didn't you?"

"Sure. The suit was ruined so I figured, why lug the thing around?"

I pulled off my own helmet and showed it to her. "You can't shut suit radios off," I said, "and their range is pretty far. If he decided to carry yours around with him in the shuttle, he could have heard every word we said."

"You mean—?"

We were both just starting to reach for our blasters when a new voice spoke up from the back of the cave.

"I wouldn't do that, if I were you. I'd hate to deliver damaged merchandise to my pal Burles."

There was a sudden light, as though he'd just uncovered a lamp, and we both saw the missing pirate seated comfortably next to the crack in the rear wall.

"I'd hoped I wouldn't have to reveal myself until Burles showed up," he glanced at a chronometer on his wrist, "which should be anytime, now, but you forced my hand. Too bad." His face, so familiar to me, grew serious. "Oh, well. Now, please, stand up, then slowly undo your belts and lower them to the floor."

I couldn't believe it. The man holding a blaster on us was Frank, the soft-spoken, shy, shuttle maintenance man.

Chapter Forty-Six

"Frank?" I said. "My God, Frank, I thought you were my friend. You were the one who taught me to fly. How can you be a pirate?"

He shrugged. "The same way you're going to be. I was shanghaied off this moon nearly thirty years ago. After a while, after I'd been on a few raids, it was too late for me to be anything else."

It was all starting to make sense now. I mean, who would make a better recruiter than the guy who gave the flying lessons? He would see the brightest and the best of the Brighthome crowd, and he was in the best position to know which shuttles to abduct, and to cover for their absences. It all made so much sense, now that it had been pointed out to me. If only I could have seen it earlier.

"Frank," I said, starting to take a step forward. He froze me with a single wave of his blaster.

"Don't do it, Tom. I'm not like the kiddies you faked out on the station. You push me, and I'll kill you."

I looked into his eyes, once, and knew he wasn't kidding.

Mikey started to move, and I knew what she was thinking: *Better to die from the blaster than let Burles get his hands on her again*, but I reached out and grabbed her arm.

"Don't do it," I said, trying to send her a message with my eyes. We had some hope—not much, but some—and, if it failed, we could always die later.

I don't know if she understood my message, but she gave me a small nod and relaxed slightly. I could tell she was still on edge, and if Frank gave her anything resembling an opening, she would make a move.

I guess that meant it was up to me to make sure he didn't give her an opening. I didn't want her to die, and I certainly didn't want her to die before all our options had played themselves out.

"So, Frank," I said, raising my voice just a little, "Burles sent his message to you. Tell me, just out of curiosity, what did it say?"

He chuckled. "Is that the best question you can come up with, Jenkins? I'd have expected something better from you. But all right," he added, after pausing to make it seem like he wasn't going to answer. "It was a short one. He couldn't say too much without the Spacers catching on, so all he said was, 'The fish got away. They're swimming for the caves. Hurry.'" He chuckled. "Again, it wasn't very impressive, but it got the job done. I'm here, aren't I?"

There wasn't much to say to that, so I switched

topics. "Frank, I've got to admit, we never suspected you. We had Pierson pegged as the pirate."

Frank laughed. It was the first time I'd heard him laugh, and it wasn't a nice sound.

"Pierson? He's a crook, all right, but he's no pirate. We pay him a bit to look the other way when we need him to, and to fill out the accident report forms properly when a ship disappears, but that's all. Between us and the little bit he scams off some of the parents, he expects to retire in a few years. We may even let him."

I hadn't expected him to answer, but as long as he felt like talking I'd keep asking. "And Forrester?" I pressed.

That didn't bring a laugh. In fact, Frank sobered right up. "Don't mention him, kid. I don't know him, and I don't want to. Talk is he's a retired Spacer, still trying to do his part to clean up the galaxy."

That surprised me. Forrester, a retired Guardsman? That was interesting. I wondered if it was true.

But I didn't want to talk about the Guard. He might not know about the *Daedalus*, but if he did I didn't want him thinking about it. "So," I asked, "how soon do you expect Burles to show up?"

Frank chuckled again. "Any time, now."

He barely got the words out before I heard Burles' voice echoing from the outer tunnel. "Come out, come out, wherever you are," he called.

Beside me, Mikey shook off my arm and tensed again, preparing to leap at Frank.

There was nothing I could do. Nothing, that is, except send up a little prayer, and hope that we'd all figured things out right.

Now, I thought. *Do it now!*

And then, as if he'd read my mind, Jamie stepped out from the crack beside Frank and laid his blaster alongside the pirate's head.

"Don't move, Frank," he said.

I started to relax, thinking that this part, at least, was all wrapped up, when I saw Frank smile. I opened my mouth to say something, but it was too late. He jerked his head backward suddenly, hitting Jamie right in the nose, and then slammed his elbow into Jamie's gut. To top it all off, he swung his own blaster at Jamie's head, even though Jamie was already sagging to his knees, all the fight taken out of him.

Frank's blaster never reached him. While I was standing there watching, Mikey was moving. She leaped almost as soon as Frank made his first move, and now she caught his arm before he could finish his blow. Moving too quickly for me to follow all of her actions, she first disarmed him, then reversed his weapon and brought it down on his head.

Frank crumpled to the floor without a sound, to lie next to a gasping and bleeding Jamie.

"Thanks, Mikey," he said when he could.

She just nodded and turned to me. "Not that I'm not glad to see him," she said, "but just where did he come from?"

I was still in shock over seeing her move like that, and it took me a moment to find my tongue.

"There's a whole network of tunnels back there," I said, pointing to the far wall. "Some of them connect with the Doorstep—that first room past the squeeze. Some of them I've never found an end to. Anyway, Jamie and I learned the back way in to this room a long time ago. We figured it might come in handy someday, but we never planned on anything like this, eh, Jamie?"

He had a hand to his nose, trying to staunch the flow of blood, but he gave me a shaky smile and a nod.

Mikey nodded, too. "Good. Is there another way out of these caves?"

At that, some of my good humor left. "No," I said. "At least not that I've ever found. As far as I know, there's only one exit, and Burles has that one blocked."

"So what do we do?" Jamie asked. "Wait for the Guard?"

"No," Mikey said. "Burles doesn't know what just happened, and he's expecting us to come out. So let's go out."

"But—" I started.

She silenced me with a look. "I'm tired of running from him, Tom. It's time to end this." After a moment, I nodded and she went on, "I'll go out first, unarmed. You two come after me, with all the blasters, including Frank's. I don't think he'll be waking up any time soon, but if he does I don't want him armed."

We nodded again, and Mikey handed us the blaster she'd taken from Frank. She put her holster back on, but gave the weapon to me. I had to agree, the empty holster was a nice, dramatic touch.

She turned, then, and gave me a quick kiss on the lips, then spun away and headed out of our campsite.

For a moment, I could only stand and look after her. What had that meant? Was it a kiss good-bye, or a promise to come back? Then I started off after her, wondering if we were doing the right thing.

Chapter Forty-Seven

When Mikey got to the squeeze, she paused and called out, "All right, Burles, we're coming out. Go easy with your blaster." In the cave beyond, Burles only chuckled, but she wasn't paying any attention to him. Instead, she turned back to me and whispered, "Give me five minutes. It should all be over by then, one way or another. Remember, five minutes, then come out with your weapons ready."

"Five minutes!" I whispered back. "Mikey, what—"

But she laid her finger on her lips, turned away, and vanished through the squeeze.

"What do you think's going on?" Jamie whispered in my ear.

"I don't know," I whispered back, but it wasn't true. I had the feeling that I knew all too well what was about to happen, and I couldn't see any way to stop it.

I could hear the sounds of Mikey squeezing through the tight space and then through the narrow tunnel beyond. A moment later, and I heard Burles chuckle again.

"Well, my dear," he said, "so nice to see you again."

"Can it, Burles," Mikey said. "I've got a proposition for you: Frank has agreed to give us five minutes to ourselves. I propose that we use that time to settle things between us."

"What are you saying?" I noticed that some of the humor had vanished from Burles' voice.

"Simple," Mikey said. "We fight it out. If I win, we walk out of here, and you never bother us again."

"And if I win?" Burles asked.

"You get me."

He chuckled again. "I've already got you."

"No," she said. "I mean you get me. No force. No coercion. You get me, fully, freely, and willingly. What do you say?"

This time he laughed outright. "I say I'd be a fool to accept your suggestion. You're a good fighter. I've seen that. You might even force me to kill you, or to maim you so badly that you wouldn't be any fun afterwards. No, little lady, I think I'll take you on my terms."

This time it was Mikey who laughed, a low, mocking sound that echoed among the rocks. "I don't blame you for being scared, Burles," she said, and there was scorn in her voice. "After all, I've beaten you both times I've faced you."

That stung him. "I was surprised both times," he said, but it was a weak comeback and he knew it. She didn't even bother to reply to it. After a moment, he said, "Fully and willingly, huh? How do I know I can trust you?"

She laughed again, but without the mockery. "Hey, you're the pirate. How do I know I can trust *you*?"

"Good point. All right," he said. "There. My blaster's holstered and the power pack's removed. Now I'll just take the whole thing off and lay it in this corner. I don't think you'll try and get it, but even if you do, you won't be able to reassemble it in time to get a shot off. Now, little lady, I guess I'm ready when you are."

That was my cue. I started through the squeeze, but Jamie caught my shoulder.

"It hasn't been five minutes, yet," he whispered.

"Do you think I'm actually going to let her fight him?" I asked. "No way. I'm going in there."

"Tom," he said. "I think she wants to."

He was right. I was pretty sure this was what she wanted, too, but that didn't mean I was going to let it happen. I shrugged off his hand and went through the squeeze, one blaster in my holster and another one in my hand.

Chapter Forty-Eight

It only took a few seconds for me to make it into the outer cave. I could picture the two of them circling, looking for an opening, and I was braced for the sound of flesh striking flesh, but it didn't come. All I could hear was their feet shuffling in the loose sand of the cave floor.

I came around the bend and into the cave and saw them, just as I had pictured them. They were both in a crouch, hands held up in front of them, and just out of arm's reach of each other.

"Burles!" I said, raising my blaster. "Freeze!"

Just as I said that, Mikey launched herself in the air. Burles' head swung toward me; I heard Mikey cry, "Tom, no!" and then I saw her try to pull her punch. She must have been successful, because even though she knocked him down, they both scrambled to their feet quickly.

"What's this?" Burles demanded.

Mikey grinned. "Added incentive. For you. I forgot to tell you, Frank's unconscious back in the caves. We have all the blasters, and there's a Space Guard ship coming to pick the two of you up."

His shoulders sagged at that. "And what of your proposition?"

She spat in the floor at his feet.

He nodded. "I thought so." He looked at his blaster, lying disassembled in one corner, and then looked back at her. "You still want to fight?"

"Mikey—" I started, but she didn't even look at me.

"You bet," she said. Then, glancing very quickly over at me, she added, "Tom, don't interfere. No matter what happens. In fact, if Burles defeats me, let him walk. That might make him try a little harder."

"Forget it, Mikey," I said.

"Tom," again she glanced at me, though I could see she didn't want to take her eyes off Burles, "please. I have to do this. Promise me, okay?"

I hesitated, but only a moment. "All right," I said reluctantly, but I wasn't certain I would keep that promise.

She flashed a smile at me. "Thanks," she said. Then, to Burles, "Well?"

He nodded. "Any time."

I switched the blaster to my left hand so that I could wipe the sweat from my palm, then switched it back as they started to circle again.

I'd seen Mikey fight a couple of times now—or at least I'd been watching a couple of times when she fought; her moves had usually been too fast for me to see—but still I wasn't prepared for what happened next.

Burles stepped in and threw a hard, fast right hand toward her midsection. I winced, knowing how hard his blows landed, but this one didn't land. I saw her put her left hand on his elbow and just kind of brush his arm to one side while her body went the other way. The next thing Burles and I knew, she was standing beside him and threw a hard blow of her own into his ribs. He grunted and grabbed for her, but she was already gone, out of his reach and circling once more.

The thing that I couldn't believe was that I knew how fast Burles was. I'd seen his blows coming before he threw them and couldn't get out of the way, yet he couldn't lay a hand on Mikey.

This went on for a couple of minutes, during which Burles must have missed Mikey five or six times and taken five or six hard body blows in return. He was starting to slow, and grunting in pain every time she hit him, when they were interrupted by the sound of a ship landing outside the cave.

"What's that?" I asked. "The *Daedalus?*"

Burles quit his endless circling to let Mikey answer.

"No," she said. "They'll still be tied up with the pirate ship. Even after the battle, there'll be a lot that needs to be done. That'll probably be a run-about from the *Daedalus*, sent here to see if we need any help. What it means, though, is that the battle itself is over, and the Guard won." She grinned, then, and I couldn't help thinking how beautiful she looked. "There's a rumor," she said to Burles, "that Old Jack himself comes out to greet the new recruits. What do you think, Burles? Could he have been on that ship that the Guard just captured?"

He didn't say anything, but the way his shoulders slumped in sudden defeat told her all she needed to know. She chuckled, and in that moment he drew his knife and threw himself at her with a great cry of rage.

I expected her to sidestep again, but she didn't. I expected her to disarm him, but she didn't do that, either. Instead, she stepped right into his charge and delivered a flurry of flashing body blows. He stopped as if he'd run into a wall. Calmly, she stepped back, then spun suddenly and brought her foot up in a crashing blow to his head.

He didn't make a sound, just folded up and dropped in a heap at her feet, and lay there unmoving. She stood over him, looking down, barely breathing hard, an unreadable expression on her face.

After a moment she looked up at me and grinned. "I shouldn't have done that," she said, "but, God, did it feel good."

Chapter Forty-Nine

Four Guardsmen came in moments later. It was the first time I'd seen actual Spacers since coming to Brighthome, and the sight of their bright blue uniforms nearly took my breath away. In that moment, all my hopes and dreams of the past four years crystallized within me. I'd fantasized about joining the Guard, I'd dreamed about it, I'd even planned for it. In that moment, my desire went beyond all of that, to a level of commitment I hadn't known I was capable of.

Ironically, none of the Guardsmen took any notice of me at all. Two of them took charge of Burles, restraining his arms before he woke up and then escorting him outside. The other two looked at Mikey.

"There's another one further in," she said. "He should still be unconscious. Jamie," she raised her voice slightly, "would you escort these two to the campsite?"

Jamie came out from the shadows at the back of the cave. The two Guardsmen checked their weapons, made eye contact with each other, and then followed Jamie into the side tunnel that eventually led to our camp.

"Well," I said, turning back to Mikey, the strength of my newfound resolve making me bold.

"Well," she said, a faint smile on her face. She wasn't going to make this easy for me, but then I guess I hadn't really expected her to.

I reached out and touched her hair. When I spoke, my voice had an edge of sadness to it. "I suppose you'll be leaving now, won't you, Alex?"

Her smile faded at that. She opened her mouth to say something, but before she could the two Guardsmen who had gone after Frank came back out of the tunnel.

"He's gone," the first one said.

"He must have gone deeper in," said the second.

Mikey sighed. "We'll talk later," she said to me, and then the three of them turned and ran out of the cave.

Chapter Fifty

I wanted to stay and watch the Guardsmen as they began their search for Frank, but they made it clear that I'd only be in the way. They took our blasters from us and then kicked the two of us out. Jamie and I went over to the cafeteria for a quick bite, then he headed back to the dorm for some rest. I didn't blame him; in fact, I felt I could use some rest myself, but there was something I needed to do first.

My decision was still glowing within me. There was nothing I could do about it until I turned eighteen—or until the Administration decided I'd turned eighteen. No one knew when I'd been born, so no one knew when my birthday was. Still, there'd come a day when I was released from Brighthome, and on that day I'd enlist in the Guard. Before then, though, I had to come to some terms with myself.

The library was not open on Sundays, but Mr. Murphy knew about my search, and how important it was to me, and had told me I could go there whenever I wanted. I went there now.

The workstation powered up quickly. It may have been out of date, but it still worked fine. In that respect, Mr. Murphy was a lot like Frank.

I called up my search parameters and all the files of data I'd downloaded over the years. There were hundreds of names listed, names of people I'd briefly thought might be me as well as people I'd ruled out immediately, and seeing them once again brought a sad smile to my lips.

Such a dream I'd had. I'd known all along that my parents weren't Guardsmen. It was a Spacer ship that found me, and Guardsmen who ran the preliminary searches on me. If I had been one of them, they'd have known it.

It felt odd, sitting there, facing that fact for the first time. It felt sad, but it felt good, too, knowing that I had the strength now to do that.

My parents weren't Guardsmen. They might have been pirates, but most likely they were just two unlucky people who got caught in the wrong place at the wrong time. And me—and this was still hard to think about—most likely I had been the victim of an intentional brainwipe.

My parents were gone, and so were my memories. They were part of the past, and I had to look toward the future now.

I took a deep breath, then reached out to the keyboard and input the instructions to delete all of my files.

"Good-bye," I said softly, though I couldn't have

said whether I was talking to my parents, my memories, or my dreams.

Then I rose, shut everything down, and headed back out to find Jamie and to wait for Mikey to find us.

Chapter Fifty-One

Coming out of the library I glanced down the hall toward the lift that led to Mr. Pierson's office and something he'd said the other day came back to me, something about putting security cameras in the caves. I'd long suspected that the staff here had some way of monitoring what went on in those caves, of course—after all, this was a detention center. It didn't make sense that there would be a place anywhere on the moon where kids could go and be totally unsupervised. I'd just ignored it as something I couldn't do anything about. And the caves had at least provided the illusion of privacy.

Now, though, I thought about that, and about Frank hiding out down there, and it seemed to me that maybe I could do something to help out the Guard. Mikey had been there with me when Mr. Pierson said that, but she'd been distracted by his hints of a bribe and might not have paid much attention. Besides, I knew the Guard was pretty much used to doing things on their own. It might not occur to them to ask the Administrator for help.

Grinning, I turned and headed toward the lift.

Clark, the student who served as the receptionist, was not at his desk, but I wasn't surprised to see a light on in Mr. Pierson's office. This was Sunday, but there was a Space Guard runabout parked outside. It wouldn't hurt Mr. Pierson at all for the Guard to see him hard at work on a weekend.

I went in without knocking.

As before, he was standing with his back to the door, looking out the window. This time, however, he turned as soon as I entered. His expression changed when he saw me, going from a mask of professional interest and courtesy to one of sudden annoyance. But I didn't let that bother me.

"Jenkins," he said. "What do *you* want."

"The caves," I said. "They're monitored, aren't they?"

He didn't answer right away. He just looked at me, and I could see that he was thinking hard. I didn't say anything to help him out. He had to know that I'd had some involvement with what had happened earlier. I'd let him decide for himself just how closely connected he thought I'd become to the Guard.

He was silent for maybe twenty seconds before he nodded and said, "Of course. Why?"

"You know that Frank, the shuttle mechanic, is one of the pirates, don't you, and that he's hiding out in the caves?"

Mr. Pierson paled at that. "No," he said quickly. "I didn't know that. I'd heard rumors, of course, but in a place like this you hear rumors about practically everyone. And I didn't know he was in the caves."

"Well, he is, and I think it would be a good thing for all of us if we could give the Guard a little more information than that, don't you, sir?"

He didn't have to think about that one for long. "Of course," he said. "Come with me."

There was a door in the back wall of his office. It looked like the door to a closet or something, but when he opened it I saw that it led to a small room with equipment lining the walls.

That was all I got to see, however.

"Stay here," Mr. Pierson said, and vanished into the room.

He was gone about three minutes. When he came back, he was a bit pale.

"He's gone," Mr. Pierson said. "I did a full scan of all the tunnels. There's nobody in there."

"Can you track him?" I asked.

Mr. Pierson shook his head. "We're set up to keep an eye on the students, not the staff members," he said. "As long as he stays out of the student sections, he could be anywhere."

I sighed. That wasn't exactly the news I'd hoped to bring to the Guard, but it was something they needed to know.

"Well, thanks for your help," I said.

He didn't say anything as I turned and walked out, and I couldn't figure out what was bugging him. It wasn't like Frank was going to get away, after all. I mean, this was Brighthome, and that was the Guard looking for him. He couldn't hide for long, and with the *Daedalus* in the system he had no chance of getting away.

Nope, nothing to worry about, but still I hurried outside to find one of the Spacers. The sooner the Guard knew about this, and the sooner Frank was in custody, the better I'd feel.

Chapter Fifty-Two

I didn't make it very far.

I had just come out of the mall and was looking around for someone in the bright blue uniform when I felt a heavy hand fall on my arm.

"Hi, kid," said a familiar voice in my ear.

I turned and saw Frank standing next to me and slightly behind me, using me to shield him from any casual onlooker. He didn't appear to have a weapon, but I knew that didn't mean anything. He certainly didn't need one to deal with me, and depending on how long he'd been out of the caves, he'd have had time to get one.

He didn't give me time to respond. He yanked on my arm, pulling me along the building and around the corner, out of sight of the campus.

"I need your help, kid," he said, releasing my arm but staying close.

I looked at him, thinking hard. I thought about

bluffing him. I thought about simply turning around and running, yelling as loud as I could. Heck, I even thought about agreeing with him and hoping that Mikey would figure out what had happened.

In the end, though, I knew I couldn't bluff him, I could tell that I wouldn't get two steps before he caught me, and I didn't think even Mikey could figure this one out in time, so all I said was, "No."

He grinned. It was not a pretty sight.

"I figured you'd say that, kid," he said. "You're braver than you think. But before you try anything stupid, let me ask you this: you still curious about who you are?"

That caught me off guard. He saw that and grinned again.

"I was on the run four years ago that hijacked the ship you were on," he said. "I know the name of that ship, and I can even give you a copy of the passenger list." He paused, growing very serious. "I was *there*, Tom. I can tell you what happened. But not here."

I looked at him. "What do you want?" I asked. I knew, or at least I thought I did, but I needed time to think.

"The Guard knows you," he said. "I need you to get me off this rock and past the patrols. Once we're safe, I'll tell you everything I know."

I didn't believe him, of course. It was too convenient. More than that, though, I didn't dare believe him. If I got my hopes up, and then was disappointed . . .

"No," I said, though my voice was not as strong as I'd have liked.

He sighed, and turned slightly to look out over

the horizon. He was still tense, however, and I didn't even think about trying to make a break for it.

"You surprise me, kid," he said after a moment. "But all right, if you're not interested in your past, then how about your future?" His right hand dipped into his pocket and brought out a small, wicked looking needler. These things weren't as powerful as blasters, but at close range they were just as deadly.

"You've got two choices, kid: you can die now being a hero, or you can be smart and maybe make it through this thing alive. What's it going to be?"

This time I had no doubt about his sincerity. I could see the desperation in his eyes, and I knew that if I didn't do as he asked he would kill me on the spot.

"All right, Frank," I said, feeling my dreams die within me. "What do you want me to do?"

Chapter Fifty-Three

Frank led me to the hangar. We took a circuitous route, avoiding any chance of being seen. I was disappointed that there was no Guardsman keeping watch at the hangar, but I wasn't really surprised. As far as they knew, Frank was still holed up in the caves—assuming, of course, that Mr. Pierson hadn't said anything to them. From what I'd seen of the Administrator, I figured that was a pretty safe bet.

I topped off the *Hobo One*'s fuel tanks while he kept watch. I glanced over to the engine compartment a few times. I still had Burles' little widget in my pocket, though I couldn't see how it would help me to reinstall the device. I was desperate, though, and clutching at straws, and probably would have reattached it if I'd had the chance.

Frank never gave me the chance. I doubted that he knew I still had it, but it was obvious that he didn't trust me. He kept a close eye on me as I worked.

When I was finished, he came over and inspected the ship, then motioned for me to lead the way. I looked over at the closest door, knowing it was now or never, but Frank kept his needler pointed right at me.

Slowly I climbed aboard, with Frank at my heels.

We didn't even make it out of the hangar before we were noticed. I had barely gotten the hangar doors open and the engine fired up when my communications panel lit up.

"Answer it," Frank said, "but remember, it's your life, too."

I nodded, but made no move toward the controls.

Frank frowned. "What's the matter?" he said. "Answer it."

"All right, but don't get nervous," I said. "I'm not very familiar with these controls, Frank. After all, it's been a long time since training. I don't want you to shoot me if I press the wrong button."

"So don't press the wrong button," he said.

Somehow, I wasn't surprised by his response.

Grimly, I reached out and opened the channel. This old runabout didn't have visual capability, but with Frank's needler pressing into my side I wouldn't have used it anyway.

"*Hobo One*," I said.

"*Hobo One*, this is the Space Guard runabout *Icarus* on station here on Brighthome. Your engines are hot, *Hobo One*. What is your situation?"

Frank dug his needler a little deeper into my side. I tried to ignore it, but he wasn't making it easy for me.

"*Icarus*, this is Tom Jenkins, regular pilot for the *Hobo One*. It's a weekend, and I wanted to take one last turn among the stars before classes resume tomorrow." I paused, then added, "Check with the Administrator; he'll vouch for me."

Frank let that one pass. I wasn't trying to get cute, but it did occur to me that Mr. Pierson would mention to them that Frank was on the loose, and they might figure things out.

But their response was immediate. "Roger, *Hobo One*. Good flying."

Which either meant that Frank was right and the Space Guard knew who I was, or that they knew he was no longer in the caves and that he was on board this ship. If they knew that, then they probably also knew that he was armed, and they were trying to devise a way to capture him without getting me killed.

"Thanks, *Icarus*," I said, praying it was the second one. "*Hobo One* out."

And then I took us out of the hangar and away from Brighthome.

Chapter Fifty-Four

Once we cleared Brighthome's gravity well, Frank took over the controls. That was too bad, but at least he put his needler away.

"You're the navigator now, Jenkins," he said. "Plot me a course back to the station."

"The station?" I said. "But I thought—"

He grinned. "Let me guess: you thought we'd either head out of the system or land on Antillus, right?"

I nodded.

"Bad ideas. For one thing, there's no place to go outside of the system. With the *Daedalus* out there, we'd have no chance of hooking up with another ship. And Antillus is just as bad; there's no way off of there."

"And there is a way off of the station?"

"Yep. That place holds tricks you haven't seen, things even Burles didn't know about. We have several places like this scattered about the various systems. Abandoned space stations, mined-out moonlets, empty asteroids, anything that'll serve as a temporary base or a place to hide when things get hot. And they all have their little surprises." He looked at me, then really looked at me, and after a moment he went on, "I'll make you a promise, kid, though I don't expect you to believe me. We make it to the station safely, and I'll leave you there, unharmed. Eventually the Guard'll show up and you can return to your life."

He was right. I didn't believe him. But I didn't see any reason to say so. I simply turned to my controls and started working on plotting the course.

I wasn't as fast as either Jamie or Mikey, but I did it. The safeguards were still off, so there was no problem. Frank watched my every move, but he made no comment, merely engaged the new course as soon as I laid it in. He kept our speed slow so that we wouldn't raise any ripples on the Space Guard's screens, but not so slow that it would take us all day to get there, either. I did a rough calculation and figured we'd arrive at the station within the hour.

Not much time to put a plan into effect. And even less considering that I had no plan, or even an idea.

"So, tell me, Frank," I said, "now that you're pretty much home free, how much of what you told me before was a lie?"

He looked over at me. "You mean about who you are?"

I nodded.

He grinned. "Actually, kid, it was the truth. I really was on that run." He must have seen how that affected me because his grin widened. "But I thought you didn't care about that."

"Tell me," I said. There was a naked plea in my voice that I didn't try to disguise. "Please."

He grew serious and shook his head. "Not yet, kid."

At that moment, if I'd had a weapon, I'd have used it not to capture Frank but to make him answer me, if only so I could tell if he was lying. I wanted to believe him, yet I was afraid to believe him.

Disgusted, I turned back to my controls.

"You might as well open the scanners," he said. "Not much we can do if the Spacers decide to come after us, but it'd be nice to know it if they do."

I nodded and slid the cover back. I'd caught just enough of Mikey's lessons to know how to activate them, even if I didn't know how to fine-tune them.

"See if you can find out anything about the Spacer cruiser out there," he said.

"Right," I said, bending over the scanner controls. If he didn't know that the *Daedalus* had captured the pirate vessel, I sure didn't want to be the one to tell him.

Not yet, anyway.

Thinking of the *Daedalus* made me wonder if they'd try to contact us also. I hoped not; they would expect Mikey to answer, and I didn't want them getting suspicious in front of Frank. On the other hand, I didn't think I had too much to worry about. They were probably still busy wrapping things up after their engagement with the pirates.

"I don't know much about these," I said. "You never taught me, remember?"

"Here," he said, reaching over and pointing at

a couple of controls. "These'll change your magnitude and the area you're scanning. Just move 'em around until you've covered all of the system."

For one brief moment, as he was leaning over like that, I had a clear shot at him. My right hand tightened into a fist, but beyond that I made no move. I didn't think I could take him out with a single shot, and I knew if I tried it and failed I was dead.

He must have sensed what I was thinking. Without saying a word, he swivelled his head at me and grinned.

I didn't say anything, either, but my right hand slowly relaxed.

He nodded, straightened up, and returned to his controls.

"System's clear," I said a few minutes later. "At least I'm not picking anything up." I had no idea if what I was saying was true or not; I couldn't read the squiggles on the screen like Jamie and Mikey could. But if I was wrong, Frank didn't say anything about it.

The rest of the trip went by slowly, but uneventfully. If the Guard was watching us, they gave no sign of it, and no one tried to communicate with us again.

"Frank," I said, as he was starting his approach, but he held up a hand to cut me off. Which was just as well since I didn't know what I was going to say. I was just nervous, I guess.

"First off, kid, now's not a good time to bug me. I don't trust those kids on the station to have the computer set up properly, so we're going in on manual. It's been a long time since I did a maneuver like this, and I'm going to need all my concentration."

I could understand that, but I didn't offer to take the controls for him.

"Second," he went on, "you're a good kid. I like you, and I'm serious about telling you what I know. But not right now. So whatever you were going to say, unless it's about the Space Guard or the integrity of that station, save it till we're docked, okay?"

I didn't say anything, and he turned back to his flying.

My hands itched for those controls. I could tell he was rusty. He was overcompensating slightly in each direction, so that we were yawing considerably as we came in. If he didn't get that under control, we were going to scrape the sides of the docking ring as we came in.

Slowly he straightened us out, but he still had us coming in too fast. I was sitting on the edge of my seat, longing to reach over and throttle us back some, but I didn't dare interfere.

When we were about fifty meters out, Frank looked over at me, grinned, and said, "Gotcha." Then he killed our speed and brought us into perfect alignment with a single move.

I couldn't help it. I grinned. Here he'd been playing with me all this time.

I sobered, then, as I realized where my thoughts were heading. I liked Frank, liked him a lot, and a part of me wanted to see him get away. The rest of me, however, knew that he was a pirate and fully expected him to kill me.

And I realized something else, too. Earlier I had committed myself to the idea of becoming a Guardsman, and then that very same day Frank had come along and stripped that idea from me. He'd threatened me, and I'd surrendered, and I knew that the Guard could never be interested in a coward.

And for that, more than anything else, I could never forgive him. He might be able to give me back my past, but he could never give me back my future.

We were about ten meters out of the station and slowing perfectly. Frank's attention was on his board, though I could see that his job was pretty much over. I didn't even think about it. I just reached over and hit the jets.

Less than half a second later we crashed hard into the side of the docking ring. Frank and I were thrown forward into our consoles. I felt a burst of pain and then I felt nothing at all.

Chapter Fifty-Five

I came to slowly and reluctantly. I was hanging against my straps and I hurt everywhere. Even breathing was painful, but I didn't think anything was broken.

Frank was another matter. His face was all bloody, and I could see bone showing through a flap of skin above his left eye. Beyond that, I couldn't tell how badly he was hurt. He looked like he was going to be out for a while yet, so I turned my attention to the ship.

The collision alarm was ringing, and it wasn't helping my head any. I killed it, then started scanning the boards.

Right away, I could see there was trouble. We had bounced off the station, and though we'd been lucky and hadn't rebounded in the direction of Antillus, we were still deep within the planet's gravity well. The engines were off-line, shut down by the computer moments after the collision, and if I couldn't get them restarted we would eventually burn up in Antillus' atmosphere.

But that wasn't our most immediate problem. This craft was ancient, and not in the best shape to begin with, and the crash had weakened a couple of the seams. So far, there were only pinhole leaks along them, but it looked like they could tear open at any moment.

Time to get into our suits.

I turned back to Frank and saw that there was another problem. His console had collapsed around him, pinning his legs. I had no way of getting him free, and I couldn't get him into a suit while he was trapped like that.

I shook my head, then winced at the sudden pain. I'd get my own suit on, then I'd figure out what to do.

The crawl back to the suit locker was torture, and getting my suit on was even worse. I felt like I'd cracked a couple of ribs, and there wasn't a part of me that moved easily or without pain.

When I'd recovered a bit, I turned back to the locker to dig out another suit, but the sound of a sharply-drawn breath made me turn back.

Frank was coming around. I hadn't even been sure he was still alive, but the old guy was tougher than I'd thought.

He sagged back in his seat, his right hand fumbling at his straps. The way he kept his left arm motionless, I assumed it was broken.

He froze, then, and some tension came back in his shoulders, and I knew he was fully awake.

"You son of a bitch," he said. He let his head flop back so that he could look at me over his right shoulder. He was all battered and bloody, and I knew that he would have killed me in that moment if he could have.

I didn't say anything at all. I just crawled over to the nearest wall, next to the hatch, and used it to climb slowly to my feet.

"Why'd you do it, kid?" he asked. His head had fallen forward again, and I was grateful that I didn't have to look at his face anymore.

"I don't know," I said, knowing it was the truth. It had been an impulse, not a rational decision. But I suspected I'd do it again.

"If it matters," he said, though I could tell it hurt him to talk, "I didn't lie to you, Tom. About anything."

I didn't know what to say to that. I started to close my eyes, just to get away from the conversation for a moment, when I noticed that his right hand was fumbling with his pocket. The same pocket where he kept the needler.

"Don't, Frank," I said, coming alert once again.

He chuckled. "Why not, kid? What are you going to do? Ram us again?"

"No," I said. He turned back to look at me, and as he did so I raised my helmet over my head, sealed it, and put my hand on the hatch.

He froze, his hand in his pocket. Then he shook his head. "Tom," he said, his voice steady, "think about what you're doing. All I want is to get my gun out so I'll have control of the situation again. You help me get aboard the space station and all will be forgiven. I'll even tell you about your parents," he added.

For a moment I was tempted, but then I shook my head. Even if he was telling the truth, I couldn't accept that offer. "No deal," I said, my voice echoing from the speakers in the cabin. "Take your hand out of your pocket, empty, and use it to call the Guard. Then I'll help you into a suit before those seals give way."

We stayed there like that, neither of us moving, neither of us sure what would happen next, for maybe two or three seconds. Then I saw him give a sad little smile and start to draw his hand out of his pocket. But his hand wasn't empty. It held the needler.

"Frank—" I said, but then he was raising the needler and I was out of time. I shut my eyes and pulled down on the lever, hard.

There was a pop, a hiss, and then a sudden rush of air as the seals, unable to stand the stress, gave way. A moment later, I opened my eyes, looked over at Frank, and almost threw up.

"Oh, Frank," I said, my voice sounding loud in my helmet. Then I collapsed onto the floor and waited for the Guard to show up.

Chapter Fifty-Six

Jamie and I were seated in the cafeteria that evening, picking at our dinners. I'd been patched up and released, and though it still hurt to breathe, the biggest pain I carried was the one inside me.

We weren't talking much. I'd told Jamie everything that had happened and he understood that I just needed some time to think.

Mikey came in as we were finishing up. She was alone, but the air of confidence she'd picked up back in the caves still hung about her like a uniform.

She looked around, saw us, and came straight over.

"What's the latest?" I asked.

"The *Daedalus* is in orbit around Antillus. They're not saying whether they've captured Old Jack or not, but I understand there are some more ships coming in for added security."

I nodded and looked away. The scenery outside

the window was as desolate as always, but it wasn't nearly as bleak as the future I was seeing.

"And you?" I turned to look at her, keeping my face impassive. "You're leaving when the *Daedalus* pulls out, aren't you?"

That brought a reaction from Jamie. "What?" he asked. "Why would she do that?"

Mikey looked at me. "You haven't told him?" she asked.

I shook my head. "Not my secret to tell."

"When did you figure it out, anyway?" she asked.

I shrugged. "Not before our first shuttle flight. I started putting the pieces together after the Communications Officer on the *Daedalus* recognized your voice."

"What?" Jamie asked again, a note of impatience creeping into his voice. "What are you talking about, Tom?"

"Jamie," I said, turning toward him, "Mikey here was never a wayward child. She's a member of the Space Guard, sent here, I believe, to help track down the pirates."

His jaw dropped. Poor Jamie. He was a whiz at computers, but understanding people would never be his strong suit.

"You're a Guardsman?" he asked.

Mikey laughed. "Yes, Jamie. Tom's right. I'm an ensign, serving aboard the cruiser *Michelangelo*, temporarily reassigned to Brighthome for special operations. Oh, and my name's not Michaela. It's Alexandria, but I go by Alex, and if you laugh I'll punch you right in the nose." She smiled when she said that last part, her eyes flicking over to me, and I knew she was thinking of the last time she said that.

"Wow," he said.

"When do you leave?" I asked.

She turned back to me. "When you said. The *Daedalus* will be pulling out when the additional ships arrive. The *Michelangelo* will be one of those ships and I'll resume my regular duties then." I didn't say anything, and after a moment she added, "A couple of days, probably."

I nodded. I didn't know what to say. I'd expected this, but hearing her say it still hurt. More than I'd thought it would.

"I see," I said. "I—"

She interrupted me. "Would you like to come along?"

"What?" Jamie and I said that together.

"Unless, of course, you *like* it here on Brighthome . . ." she added.

"Wait, Mikey," I said. "I mean, Alex. What are you talking about?"

She looked at me and suddenly she was very serious. "I'm talking about your future, and about both of you making a difference."

"No," I said, and both of them turned to look at me. "Don't you understand," I said, "Frank beat me. He threatened me, and I did what he wanted." I turned away, looking back out the window. "I'm a coward, and there's no place for cowards in the Guard."

She reached out and touched my hand. "You're right, Tom," she said. "The Guard isn't looking for cowards, but it isn't looking for fools, either. You did the intelligent thing. You went along when you had to, when you knew your death wouldn't help things, but you resisted every chance you could. You did everything a good Guardsman would have done."

I turned to look at her, and saw that she was sincere. I don't know what emotion she saw in my eyes, but she didn't look away.

After a moment, I nodded.

"Good," she said. "Come with me."

Jamie and I looked at each other, but neither of us said a word. Together we rose and followed her outside.

I figured she was going to take us to the Space Guard runabout parked outside the caves. It was the only thing that made sense given the hints she'd dropped.

I was wrong. She took us to the building where most of the classes were held. There were no students around. It was Sunday, after all, but even if it had been a school day, none of the kids were likely to get much studying done with that runabout sitting on the ground a few hundred meters away.

She led us to Mr. Forrester's room, the very classroom where I'd first taken notice of her. The door was shut, but there was a light on behind it, and she walked right in without knocking.

Mr. Forrester was sitting behind his desk reading something on his computer display. When we came in he turned the display off and rose to his feet.

He still looked tough, but I thought I caught a glimpse of warmth peeking out around the edges, like the light shining out from around his door.

"Alex," he said, nodding toward her. "Gentlemen. What can I do for you?"

"Sir," she said, "I'd like to sponsor these cadets for admission into the Space Guard. I'm here to ask for your permission and your support."

He looked at her for a moment, and then shifted

his gaze to us. His eyes were stern and intense, and it was clear that he was very serious. "Are you sure about this, Ensign?" he asked.

She nodded. "Absolutely, sir. I've shipped with both of these men, and I can say that they would both make fine additions to the Guard."

He smiled, then, and his whole attitude softened. "I know, Ensign. I've been watching these two myself, and hoping for something like this. But," he added, "it's really up to them."

I couldn't believe this was happening. It was all too sudden to make sense of. Even though I'd figured it out, sort of, it was still too much for me to take in.

Jamie and I looked at each other. Mikey—Alex—hadn't given us a chance to talk this over. We both knew that this was what I wanted, but was it right for Jamie? Only he could answer that, and I had no idea what his answer would be.

"Tom," he said, "does this mean Frank was right? Mr. Forrester really is a retired Guardsman?"

Mr. Forrester chuckled, but it was Alex who answered.

"Frank was half right, Jamie. Mr. Forrester is a Guardsman, but he's not retired. In fact, he's a full Colonel. The Guard put him here, and then leaked the rumors about him, figuring that the pirates would be more confident if they thought they knew where the Spacer spy was. Then they sent me here."

I nodded. I hadn't figured that part out, but it made sense.

"So," she asked. "What's it going to be?"

I looked at Jamie. He looked at me, and for a moment I couldn't tell what he was going to do. Then he grinned and nodded.

I grinned, too. "Where do we sign, sir?" I asked.

The colonel produced some papers for us, and said, "It occurs to me that, as wards of the state, Mr. Pierson will need to sign these as well. Will that present a problem?"

Again it was Alex who answered. "I don't think so, sir." I didn't have to look at her to know she was smiling. "I'm sure Mr. Pierson will be more than happy to oblige."

"Fine," the colonel said. Turning his attention back to us, he went on, "You'll report to the *Michelangelo* when she arrives. You'll serve aboard her for a probationary period. The Ensign here has chosen to sponsor you; she'll be responsible for your training while you're on board. When each of you reaches the age of eighteen, you will be admitted into the Academy as full cadets. Any questions?"

"No, sir," I said, and Jamie echoed me.

We signed the papers, and as we did so it occurred to me that this wasn't just a dream come true for me, it was a new home for Jamie and myself.

I looked at him and grinned. "Welcome home, buddy," I said. "Welcome home."

DAVID WEBER

Honor Harrington (cont.):

Field of Dishonor

Honor goes home to Manticore—and fights for her life on a battlefield she never trained for, in a private war that offers just two choices: death—or a "victory" that can end only in dishonor and the loss of all she loves....

Other novels by DAVID WEBER:

Mutineers' Moon

"...a good story...reminds me of 1950s Heinlein..."
—*BMP Bulletin*

The Armageddon Inheritance

Sequel to *Mutineers' Moon*.

Path of the Fury

"Excellent...a thinking person's Terminator."
—*Kliatt*

Oath of Swords

An epic fantasy.

with STEVE WHITE:

Insurrection
Crusade

Novels set in the world of the Starfire ™ game system.

And don't miss Steve White's solo novels,
The Disinherited *and* **Legacy!**

continued ☞